ONCE UPON A SCREAM
Twisted Fairy Tales From The Dark Side

I0551891

Edited by Dorothy Davies

ONCE UPON A SCREAM
Twisted Fairy Tales From The Dark Side

GRAVESTONE PRESS

CONTENTS

We're Ugly and We Own It

David Turnbull

"You know what they call us, don't you?" said Grizelda, applying copious amounts of rouge to her cheeks.

Euphemia nudged her sister to one side to steal a better share of the mirror. "Who are *they*?"

"Absolutely everyone who's anyone," replied Grizelda, nudging vigorously to regain her lost territory. "The *ugly* sisters. That's what they call us."

Euphemia froze holding a false eyelash between her thumb and her forefinger like a stiff dead spider. She turned to her sister. "*Ugly*?"

Grizelda nodded solemnly.

"We're not ugly!" cried Euphemia, glancing cautiously at her reflection from the corner of her eye.

"I know," said Grizelda. "How ridiculous is that?"

"At least they haven't forgotten us completely," said her sister. "At least they still talk about us."

"I suppose that is some sort of consolation," agreed Grizelda. "But when was the last time we received an invited to a ball or a banquette?"

"Who cares," huffed Euphemia. "If an invitation arrived today, I don't think I'd even bother to open it."

7

Grizelda caught the nostalgic look in her sister's tear-filled eye. "You miss it all as much as I do."

Euphemia nodded, stifling a sob. "Those were the days, sister."

They both fell into a subdued silence.

***

"I've been thinking," said Grizelda later, as they sat by the fireside, sipping cups of sweet tea and toasting muffins. "The only reason anyone remembers us at all is because *she* is our stepsister."

"I suppose," agreed Euphemia. "Once *she* gets herself pregnant, we're going to be forgotten altogether. People go just as crazy about a royal birth as they do about a royal wedding – even if they do end up paying more taxes to cover all the pomp and ceremony of the Christening."

Grizelda blew on her tea and took a rather unladylike gulp. "You think?"

"I know," said Euphemia.

"It's going to be simply awful then," moaned Grizelda.

"Unless we do something."

"Like what?"

"Keep their attention. Move the focus back to where it belongs. Make sure they can't forget us."

"How?"

"There are things we could do."

"Like what?" asked Grizelda and polished off her tea.

Inexplicably Euphemia started to snigger.

"What?"Grizelda asked again.

Euphemia's snigger turned to an uncontrolled giggle. Her shoulders jerked up and down. Her plump, powdered bosoms jiggled as she pointed at Grizelda's face.

"What?" demanded Grizelda. "What is it?"

"Take a look at yourself," said Euphemia.

Grizelda stood up and looked at herself in the mirror above the fireplace. Her lipstick had smeared over her face, giving her lips an oddly lopsided look. She pulled out her handkerchief and began to dab it away. "Thank God no one saw. They really could have called me *ugly* with good reason."

"That's it!" cried Euphemia.

"What?" cried Grizelda.

"Where do you keep your razor?"

Euphemia had leapt to her feet and was pacing impatiently up and down.

"My razor?" asked Grizelda, affecting a confused look.

"The one you use to shave the stubble on your chin," said Euphemia.

Grizelda looked mortally offended. "I do *not* have stubble on my chin."

"But you do have a razor though," insisted Euphemia.

Grizelda accepted defeat.

"It's beside the mug in the bathroom."

"Go fetch it!" said Euphemia. "We're going to shave our heads!"

"Why ever would we do that? We'll look…"

Euphemia waited for the penny to drop.

Grizelda blinked.

"*Ugly*!" she cried.

"Exactly!" said Euphemia. "They want *ugly*, we'll damned well give them *ugly*."

***

That afternoon they pranced through the market square - bald as coots - sunlight sparkling against their shiny, shaven heads. Neither of them had been all that proficient with the razor, so they both had smatterings of crusty red nicks littering their scalps. The added drama and mystery of these minuscule wounds caused heads to turn as they passed by.

Little gossiping clusters of young ladies formed in their wake. *What had happened? Who had done this? Were they afflicted with some sort of terrible malady that had caused all their hair to drop out?* The sisters weren't telling. Painted lips pressed smugly together as they smirked surreptitiously to each other.

On Grizelda's urging they stopped a while by a hat stand and teased everyone into thinking that they were about to make purchases to cover their audacious baldness. Then they moved on, strolling down one side of the market and back up the other, gathering a burgeoning perfumed posse that matched their every step.

At last, when they were sure they'd done enough to set tongues wagging, they turned to make their departure – knowing, without a single glance backwards, that absolutely everyone was talking about them.

They sashayed back home, so engrossed by their own conceit they remained completely oblivious to the conditions which prevailed for the ordinary townsfolk. The filthy hovels the poor lived in, the beggars – crippled and blind from disease, the poverty stricken mothers with bawling babes in their arms and malnourished kids at their feet, the bent and consumptive old men.

"If I had my way you'd be tarred and feathered as well as having your heads shaved," said a voice from behind.

They swung around to find themselves face to face with a fiery looking woman. Thicket of unruly red hair, wild blue eyes, grimy overcoat, hem in tatters about her knees. She carried a bundle of pamphlets bearing the image of Till Eulenspiegel, the trickster who was fomenting insurrection and revolutionary fervour amongst the masses.

"You know why they call you the ugly sisters?" the woman spat. "Because you're ugly in here." She jabbed a grimy finger against the front of her head. "And in here." She thumped a fist against her chest. "Just like all of the pampered classes."

"How dare you speak to us like that!" Euphemia spat back. "Do you know who our sister is?"

"Hah," sneered the woman, tossing her head. "You weren't calling her your sister when she was cleaning out the cinders. Pity she's she forgotten where she came from. From where I'm standing, she's become pretty damn ugly on the inside too."

"We could have you hung for treason," said Grizelda.

"Day will come when you and all your kind will swing from nooses," said the woman, jerking her hand above her head as if pulling on a rope.

"Come on, sister," said Euphemia. "Ignore her. She's mentally afflicted."

Together they hurried away.

"Go on," yelled the woman. "Run home to mummy and daddy. Do you know how many of these people could have a roof over their heads in that big house?

***

By the time they reached home they had pushed the incident to the back of their minds. It wasn't important to them. What was important was the impact their attention-grabbing stunt had on the real people. The people who actually counted, rather than the unwashed masses.

"That was brilliant!" cried Grizelda, hanging her coat behind the door.

"Exceptional!" agreed Euphemia. "Did you see the looks on their faces?"

Grizelda nodded. "We're the talk of the town."

"All thanks to me," said Euphemia.

"To you?"

"Of course," said Euphemia, running her hand over her scabby baldness. "It was my idea."

"Was not!"

"Was too! I came up with the entire plan!"

"Did not!"

"Did too!"

"Liar!"

12

Euphemia's face turned purple. "Who are you calling a liar?" she screamed. "Who was it that told you to go and fetch your razor?"

"Well, I'm the *ugliest* for sure!" Grizelda yelled back. "It was mostly me they were looking at!"

"Was not!"

"Was too!"

The sound of something being pushed through the letterbox and landing on the doormat made them both turn round. They looked down at the gold embossed envelope at their feet.

"Did we just have a right old ding-dong?" asked Grizelda.

"I reckon we did," replied Euphemia.

"Felt good, didn't it?" sighed Grizelda. "Just like the old days."

"Better than good," agreed Euphemia, picking up the envelope.

She tore it open with her varnished thumbnail and pulled out the scented pink card. She coughed to clear her throat and then read the words on the card.

Miss Henrietta Montague
Requests the company of the sisters
Euphemia and Grizelda
on the occasion of her 21st birthday
Tonight - 7.30pm
RSVP

"Why did she put your name first?" complained Grizelda.

13

"Never mind that," said Euphemia, waving the card in her face. "You know what this means, don't you?"

Grizelda shrugged her shoulders.

"We're back, sister!" cried Euphemia. "People want to see us! People want to be seen *with* us!"

Grizelda brushed the card away with the back of her hand.

"You're not considering accepting, are you?"

"Why wouldn't we?"

"I can't stand Henrietta Montague. She's a stuck-up little floozy."

Euphemia folded the card.

"Henrietta Montague is in with the *in* crowd," she said firmly.

"You were the one who said she wouldn't even open an invite if one arrived!" spat Grizelda.

"I've changed my mind," said Euphemia.

"Well, I most certainly will not be coming with you!"

"Oh, yes you will!"

"Oh, no I won't!"

"I'm replying right now," insisted Euphemia, barging past her sister. "I'm going to accept on behalf of both of us."

"No, you won't!" yelled Grizelda, making a grab for the card. "Don't you dare put my name on that reply!"

"Will too!" screeched Euphemia, fighting her off.

They wrestled and tussled along the hall. Finally, Euphemia broke free and made a dash for the drawing room. Grizelda gave chase spluttering with fury. Barely an inch ahead of her, Euphemia slammed the door. There was a loud crash, followed by a howl of agony from the hallway.

Somewhat guiltily Euphemia opened the door a crack and peeked out. Grizelda was doubled over, hands covering her face, blood gushing through the spaces in her fingers. "You *slabbed* the door in by face," she groaned nasally. "I think *you'b* broken by *dose*."

"Oh my God!" cried Euphemia. "I'll fetch a towel. Hold your head back. No - wait. You'll choke on the blood if you do that. Hold your head forward. Is that right? I can never remember. Is it backwards or forwards for a nosebleed?"

"S*hud ub*," whimpered Grizelda, oozing all over the carpet. "*Ged* a towel before I bleed to death."

***

Half an hour later, when the seemingly limitless flow of blood had been staunched and her face had been cleaned up, Grizelda examined the damage in the mirror. Her nose had been flattened and knocked into a horrible, crooked mess.

"I'll need an operation to get this straightened," she cried in dismay.

"Perhaps not," said Euphemia.

"You think I should leave it like this? Are you mad?"

"Not mad," replied Euphemia. "Just pragmatic enough to see the advantage the situation affords."

15

"What's pragmatic about looking like this?" demanded Grizelda. "I'm …"

As before Euphemia waited for the penny to drop.

"*Ugly*!" finished Grizelda. The light went on in her head. She turned to face her reflection in the mirror again. "I'm *ugly*!" She ran her fingers over the crumpled ridges of her malformed snout. "I'm pig *ugly*!"

"Exactly," said Euphemia. "If you thought the reaction in the market was good, just think what it'll be like when you turn up at Henrietta Montague's party looking like some old sow fresh from the pigsty."

Grizelda marveled at the grotesque disarray of her nose. "I'm by far the *ugliest* now," she said triumphantly. "I've inched considerably ahead of you in the *ugly* stakes."

"Not for long," interrupted Euphemia. "Go fetch the steak hammer."

"The steak hammer?"

Euphemia nodded. "I want you to give me a damned good whack!"

***

They stole the show at Henrietta Montague's party. Everyone who was anyone wanted to be seen standing somewhere within close proximity of the celebrated *ugly* sisters. They were gossiped to and gossiped about. They gossiped back - about anyone and everyone and each other. It was just like the old days. Only ten times better.

When Henrietta Montague stepped up to cut her gigantic gaudily iced 21st birthday cake, not one person was looking at her. All eyes were fixed on the two sisters - with their bald, crusty heads - Grizelda with her painfully misshapen nose - Euphemia with a huge purple bump on her forehead that looked like a half-grown rhinoceros horn.

Outside in the cold an unsightly huddle of local urchins pressed their snotty noses and grimy hands against the glass of the window and bawled with the most inappropriate indignation when they witnessed great, creamy leftover chunks of the indulgent birthday cake being tossed wantonly into the bins, ready to be fed to the swine.

A woman with wanton red hair approached them.

"Gather round, children," she said. "Let me tell you my plan and show you how we can all eat cake."

***

Things snowballed. Wax sealed envelopes came pouring through their letterbox in a flood. Invitation cards piled up in the drawing room. Their eyes stung from reading the fine, embossed lettering on the invitations. Their arms ached intensely from writing acceptance notes. They had to construct a huge, convoluted wall chart to keep track of their all their various social engagements.

"This is a hard old slog," Grizelda complained.

"I know," empathized Euphemia. "It's a pity we don't have anyone to push around anymore."

17

"Poor us," sighed Grizelda. "If it carries on like this, we're going to have to get up really early. Like midday or something."

"And look at what it's doing to my poor hands," whimpered Euphemia. She held up her finger to show the tiny paper cut she'd suffered whilst attempting to open a particularly stubborn envelope. "Not to mention all the effort we have to go to in order to keep ahead of the game."

Ugliness they'd found could not be left as a static thing. If it wasn't varied and adjusted at regular intervals the novelty simply wore off. And it didn't do to turn up at too many functions with same old unsightly features.

So, they put Grizelda's razor to good use. Off came their eyebrows for one thing. Sometimes they shaved their scalps smooth, opening and re-opening the small, crusted nicks in the process. On other occasions they allowed a couple of days; growth of hard stubble to accumulate. Once they even left stubble on one half of their heads and shaved the other half.

Their arguments became alarmingly frequent and increasingly ferocious. They went at each other tooth and nail - clawing, biting, kicking and punching. More often than not they attacked one another with whatever was to hand. Vases and brass ornaments. Rolling pins and pokers.

The end results saved them a great deal of mental effort in coming up with new disfigurements. It was astounding how many variations there could be of black eyes and cauliflower ears, split lips and abrasions. Of course, they had to acquire a limitless supply of salves and ointments to sooth the constant throbbing of their wounds and still each morning they awoke to find their faces stuck to the dried blood on their pillows.

But then again, the attention and adulation of their peers proved a welcome distraction from the increasingly cantankerous and belligerent mood of the common people, who seemed for some unknown reason to be getting *uncommonly* uppity of late.

***

"That stings!" moaned Grizelda, bleeding from a severe head wound after one particularly vicious altercation.

Euphemia was picking shattered bits of a glass fruit bowl out of the side of her head. "No pain. No gain," she said.

On the wall opposite their house, stark red graffiti challenged the Monarchist engineered lie that the revolutionary firebrand who the people looked to as their champion was long dead. *"Tell Eulenspiegel Lives!"* it read. With far more important matters to occupy their thoughts, the sisters firmly shut the implication of this declaration from their minds.

There came the clatter of the letterbox and the familiar thump of an envelope landing on the doormat. Both sisters leapt to their feet and fought each other through the doorway, desperate to see the detail this latest invite.

It was Grizelda who reached it first. Her hands trembled as she held it up. "Look!" she said, pointing at the blob of red wax that contained the Royal seal. "It's from the Palace!"

"Let me see that!" yelled Euphemia, snatching it from her.

"Hey!" snapped Grizelda. "I got it first!"

"Let's not fight," said Euphemia. "You're already dripping blood all over the place."

Each holding the envelope by a corner they tore it open together and read the invite out loud in unison.

The Prince and Princess
Request the company of the sisters
Euphemia and Grizelda
On the Occasion of their
First Wedding Anniversary
8pm
This Evening at The Palace
RSVP

"They put your name first!" wailed Grizelda. "Why do people always do that?"

"Never mind," said Euphemia. "You know what this means, don't you?"

Grizelda shook her head, still seething at the order of the names on the invite.

"We've arrived, sis!" cried Euphemia. "We're back on the *A* list!"

"Aren't we just," gushed Grizelda, quickly forgetting the slight against her importance in the pecking order. "Whatever are we going to wear?"

"First we need to see to ourselves," said Euphemia.

"We do?"

"Of course. We can't just go to the palace looking like we have done at every other function. We have to go to town this time. We have to pull out all the stops. We want people to be looking at us and not *her*."

"Revenge?" grinned Grizelda. "I like the sound of that."

"We'll need the hammer and the pliers," replied Euphemia. "And the razor."

"The razor?" cried Grizelda. "We already shaved out heads this morning."

"Not to shave with," said Euphemia. "This time I reckon we're going to have to lop a few bits off!"

***

The Palace ballroom glimmered from the blazing candlelight of a dozen crystal chandeliers as the sisters glided across the marble floor, weaving as serenely as they could muster in and out of the Lords and the Ladies and the fops and the debutantes.

Outside there was a terrible din. Someone said this was being caused by a mob of ungrateful ruffians who were threatening to burn down the Palace and overthrow the monarchy. It was such an annoying distraction, but when a battalion of the Palace guard was dispatched, the rabble were soon thankfully silenced and dispersed by several thunderous volleys of gunfire.

The sisters hoped this would allow attention to focus on their ruthlessly self-afflicted handiwork. They had sliced off their ears and sewn them back on, facing the wrong way. Teeth had been pulled with the aid of the pliers, giving them a gaping, gummy look when they grinned. They had each endured so many thumps on the head with the hammer that their bald scalps were left looking like surging mountain ranges. They had slashed deep, furrowed scars across each other's faces and stitched them together with thick black darning thread.

There should have been cries of amazement - screams of astonishment - scandalized gasps of disbelief. Instead, there was a nothing but a depressing lack of acknowledgement.

The band played on with boisterous aplomb and at the end the piece there came the obligatory round of exaggerated bows and curtseys. It was then that they noticed the monstrously gruesome disguises that each of the guests wore. No wonder they were not managing to turn a single head. The sisters made a beeline for the punch bowl.

"I didn't realise this was supposed to be a masked ball," complained Grizelda, dipping her cup into the punch bowl for the fourth time in a row. "*She* could have mentioned the fact on the invite."

"I know," agreed Euphemia. "But by the look of some of the masks, we've been an inspiration to their design."

"We have?" cried Grizelda, plunging her cup into the punch bowl again.

Euphemia nodded, sipping at her own cup. "The physically grotesque seems to be a central theme."

"It'll be me then," said Grizelda. "People usually follow my lead."

"Shut up!" spat Euphemia. "What are you talking about?"

"Most of the masks will be based on me," said Grizelda. "I'm an inspiration to all who see me."

"In your dreams!"

"Am too!"

"No, you're not!"

What looked set to deteriorate into a full-blown fistfight was quickly defused by the approach of two rather portly looking and hideously masked gents inviting them to dance. Grizelda downed another cup of punch and followed her partner back to the floor. "Wait till the masks come off," she called back to Euphemia. "Then we'll see who gets the most looks."

"We will," agreed Euphemia. "And it certainly won't be you. That's for sure!"

***

The Palace clock struck the first stroke of midnight. The band fell silent. The guests counted down the gongs. *She* made her entrance, gliding down the marble stairwell, linked arm in arm with the Prince. Her dress was exquisite - silk and fine lace and brocade – the famous glass slippers encased her dainty feet. Her hair had been expertly

23

styled into a sophisticated and complicated beehive, with delicate little pearl beads dotting its curvature.

But her face was a sight to see.

She had obviously been involved in some terrible accident. Her skin seemed to have been shredded and sliced. It hung down in meaty flaps around her face, exposing muscle tissue, sinew and white bone.

"I'm glad you both came," she slurred through her raggedy lips, when finally she reached the place where they had been bustled into line with the other *ladies*. "Let bygones be bygones, that's what I say."

"What happened to you?" asked Grizelda, eyeing her stepsister's innumerate wounds.

"Isn't it the end?" she gushed in response. "I had it done especially for this evening. You'll have noticed that the Prince has matching mutilations. We're both in terrible agony. But you know what they say..."

"No pain. No gain," interjected Euphemia.

Their stepsister let out a coy giggle and nodded her agreement.

"I've no idea where these things start," she said. "But disfigurement is definitely all the rage this season. One must keep up with fashion trends when one is in the public eye you know."

She leaned in and studied their addled faces.

"I can see that there's no need to explain that to either of you," she said. "Whom on earth did you go to?"

"Go to?"

"Don't tell me you did that all by yourselves? Poor dears. You should have come to me. I would

24

have lent you some money to go to a professional. Disfigurement parlors are opening up all over the Kingdom you know."

"They are?" asked Grizelda.

Her stepsister nodded and a hunk of shredded flesh fell from her chin to splat wetly on the marble floor. Grizelda and Euphemia looked along the line of Lords and Ladies and realized with a horrified gasp that none of the guests were actually wearing masks. The misshapen deformities, distorted defects, the bruises, the lesions and the scars were all too atrociously real. Everyone, it seemed, had jumped on the bandwagon.

"I'll let you both into a secret," said their stepsister, conspiratorially/ "This was a trial run, but I'm absolutely determined to set a new trend for the coming season. Amputation, my dears, is going to be the next hot thing. I'm torn between losing an arm or a leg."

A hooded figure appeared with a huge axe slung lazily over his broad shoulder.

"The royal executioner," explained their stepsister with a wink of her mutilated eye. "Poor thing. He's been over worked recently, what with all the upheaval going on amongst the commoners. But I simply couldn't let him go home tonight without putting his skills to some practical use."

In the middle of the ballroom floor a gaggle of emaciated serfs with manacles around their ankles were straining to push a heavy wooden block into place. The Prince came sidling up to where the three of them were standing. His nose was broken. There was heavy bruising around his eyes. His chin seemed to jut at an awkward angle.

"Have you decided yet, darling?" he asked.

"An arm, I think," replied their stepsister. "I don't think I could be bothered being carried around everywhere in a sedan."

"You are sure you want to do this?"

She nodded. "It's expected. People look to me as their role model. It simply wouldn't do if I wasn't ahead of the game."

With that she marched to the middle of the dance floor, her grotesquely disfigured guests hurriedly clearing a path for her. She placed her lily-white arm on the chopping block. The executioner raised his axe and brought it down with consummate professionalism.

The severed arm flopped flaccidly to the marble floor; Princess Cinderella let out a single high-pitched scream and fell into a faint. She was carried out to rancorous cheering from her guests who, in turn, became drenched in the blood that sprayed relentlessly from the cleanly sliced stump above her elbow. Pandemonium quickly broke out as everyone pushed and shoved and jostled to be next in line for the chop.

Meanwhile, over in the corner, ignored and unnoticed, Euphemia and Grizelda began to bicker and squabble amongst themselves.

"This all your fault," snapped Euphemia.

"It is not," countered Grizelda.

"Is too!"

From outside the Palace there came the angry sound of the insurgent mob regrouping. This time they had guns of their own. Euphemia lolled her head to one side and stuck out her tongue, raising her arm above her head as if she was yanking a rope.

"Whatever are you doing now?" asked Grizelda,

"Trying to see how ugly I might look swinging from the end of a noose," replied Euphemia.

A hail of bullets shattered the ballroom windows. Several of the guests dropped dead.

Alternate Endings

Rie Sheridan Rose

If Cinderella had kicked
the glass slipper
into the gutter and shattered it,
would the prince have found her anyway
or would she have served her
stepmother until one of them
died?

If Sleeping Beauty had kept
her hands to herself
and not played with the spindle,
would she have married the boy next door
and learned to spin when it was more
convenient?

If Snow White hadn't answered
the witch's knock
but kept baking bread
for the dinner she had planned that evening
would she have lived
happily ever after as a dwarven den
mother?

If Little Red had dyed
her red cloak green
and slipped past the wolf,

would she have moved in with Gramma
and helped with chores around the
house?

If Hansel hadn't had
a sweet tooth
and coaxed his sister to nibble on her house
might the witch have taken them in
and given up her wicked
ways?

So many paths that could have forked.
So many roads not taken.
Alternate endings around the corner
from how the story goes...

Wicked Heart

Gina Easton

Scabadenia was her name and she was as beautiful as the summer sky at twilight, when the day reaches up to greet the night with a kiss that spawns the colours of shadow. Dusky indigos, deep sapphires bloom and chase away the last burnished orange and gold rays of the sun and the night holds the world in its velvet grasp. The girl's eyes held all of these colours and more, every hue of the rainbow imaginable, so that they glittered like fiery jewels from their onyx depths. She was the fairest maiden in the land, of that there was no doubt.

Her mother, Queen Elinore, heard the name whispered in a dream the night before her daughter's birth. She had no idea from whence it came, but dared not risk ignoring such a message, should it prove perilous to the kingdom if a significant portent was disregarded. Therefore, despite her misgivings at the less than mellifluous sound of the name, Elinore informed her husband, King Deadfoot, that their daughter should be called 'Scabadenia'. Having been blessed { or perhaps cursed} with an unusual moniker himself, the king readily acquiesced to his wife's wishes.

Scabadenia was a loved and pampered child, much praised for her beauty and accomplishments. She was somewhat of a musical prodigy, mastering the harpsichord and lute by the age of three. By six she was a gifted seamstress and created finely-woven delicate gowns on the loom designed for her by expert artisans commissioned by the king. Her life was one of privilege and leisure, free of the hardships and rigours faced daily by the kingdom's subjects. King Deadfoot was considered a fair and honest monarch; nevertheless people were obliged to toil long days to earn their living. They were an agrarian society and planted many different kinds of crops, all requiring close attention and care. A smaller portion of the farms was designated for livestock production, to ensure sufficient food was available for the kingdom's needs. Fortunately, the present time was peaceful and prosperous and people were contented with their lot.

The young princess knew nothing of these concerns. Due to her exalted status she was forbidden any playmates who were not of royal lineage which, because of the relative isolation of their realm, left her virtually friendless. However, the attention of her doting mother more than compensated for that lack. Mother and daughter spent their days arranging and attending elaborate tea parties in the nursery. Just the two of them, along with Scabadenia's array of dolls. What Elinore did not know was that, when she was alone, Scabadenia's dolls would come to life and behave like real playmates. They would sip their tea and nibble daintily at the little frosted cakes Scabadenia provided and they would join in merry conversations with her.

Scabadenia, you see, was a witch. Not a good one. In fact, her soul was every bit as scabby as her

31

name would imply. The name, which had been whispered to the queen by an evil spirit, was from an ancient and forbidden tongue. Roughly translated, Scabadenia meant "wicked heart". Queen Elinore, of course, had been completely ignorant of this knowledge, which enabled the evil to take hold in the tiny soul of the babe she carried in her womb.

Because she was a smart as well as nasty witch, Scabadenia kept her magic a secret from everyone. She quickly tired of the insipid and patently limited conversational ability of her dolls, so she gravitated to the world outside her home. She embarked on an exploration of the beautiful forest abutting the castle grounds. Few people knew that the forest was enchanted, but with her witchy nature Scabadenia recognized it at once for the treasure it was.

Using her skills, she was able to locate the fairy folk who dwelt in secret within the lush green depths. With the utmost patience the young princess coaxed them from their hiding places, tempting them with some of the frosted cakes left over from the tea parties, {having realized that the fairies' weakness was their fondness for sweets}. When she finally succeeded in gaining their trust she spent many a happy hour devising devilish ways in which to torture and maim the little folk. One day, in desperation, they vacated the forest, taking their enchantment with them. No-one understood why all the trees and plants withered and died, their rich greenery turning to ashy grey and brown. Or why the sweet bird-song was abruptly silenced, the myriad woodland creatures vanished. No-one that is, except Scabadenia. In her black heart she rejoiced at the ravages of destruction.

The child was so irredeemably rotten that when, at the age of four, she was informed by a happy glowing Queen Elinore that she was soon to become a big sister to a new sibling, Scabadenia fumed with indignation. How dare her parents think they could do this to her! The last thing she wanted was a brother or sister to usurp her rightful position as darling of the family. In Scabadenia's warped little mind there was no room for a rival. She was the only one deserving of all their love and attention.

When Elinore miscarried, all her subjects mourned the tragic loss with their queen. Except for Scabadenia. She was so overjoyed at the success of her abortive spell that she continued to use it for her mother's subsequent pregnancies, causing five miscarriages in all. Heartbroken from the losses, grieving for the children who never drew breath, wracked with guilt for failing to provide a sibling for her only child, the queen took to her bed. A depression descended upon her, so deep and dark it buried her alive. Elinore never emerged from that black tomb of despair, succumbing eventually to unrelenting sorrow and a shattered heart.

King Deadfoot grieved the demise of his beloved wife, but knew he must be brave and stalwart for his equally beloved daughter. At fifteen, Scabadenia was a vision to behold. It was rumoured that she could dazzle a man with one glance from her jewel-tone eyes. It was certainly true that all the males of the realm grew tongue-tied, bumbling and stumbling like half-wits in her presence. Scabadenia was acutely cognizant of her charms and, for a while, she enjoyed toying with the courtiers who came and went from the castle. Their frank adulation and devoted fawning afforded her a transient amusement. However, eventually she grew bored of the constant slavish attention, irritated at the tedium it engendered. She longed for some new interest to occupy her mind.

Her father was about to oblige her in that regard. Not long after Elinore's death, King Deadfoot took Scabadenia aside. "Daughter, the time of your betrothal is at hand. I have arranged for you to marry Prince Harcourt, the only son of King Jasper. By all accounts the prince is a fine young man and the alliance would be beneficial for both kingdoms although I shall be loath to see you depart." He smiled fondly at his princess.

Scabadenia, for her part, smiled sweetly back, while inwardly sighing. She had known the day would come when she would be required to leave her home and live with the husband selected for her. She understood her royal duty, the expectation that she and Prince Harcourt would one day claim the thrones of both their realms. And that circumstance suited her ambitions just fine. For, above everything, Scabadenia desired power. Yes, one day she would rule alongside her husband, only Scabadenia had no intention of letting nature take its course. King Jasper might *appear* robust, but one spell from his daughter-in-law would take care of that.

Accordingly, Scabadenia and her trusted maidservant {whom she had rendered mute to ensure her lifelong discretion} set out on the journey that would take seven days and nights. A carriage with a brace of sturdy horses was readied to carry them through the vast forests and over mountains that separated the two realms. The journey, though long and wearying, was uneventful and they arrived at the castle of King Jasper in the early morning of the eighth day.

After a period of repose and refreshment the young bride-to-be was presented to the king. Jasper was suitably impressed by her great beauty. "My dear, you are even lovelier than has been reported. I understand you are as clever as you are beautiful. Your many accomplishments are well-known. You shall make a splendid wife for my son."

Scabdenia played her role exquisitely, smiling modestly up at the monarch as she curtsied before him but in the scheming cesspool of her mind she had already formulated a plan for getting rid of the old king. Her husband would ascend to the throne with his radiant queen at his side.

Her introduction to Prince Harcourt was an experience out of the ordinary. He was a handsome lad, quick-witted, serious as befit a future monarch, but with a good sense of humour. He was kind and considerate and demonstrated admirable prowess in hunting, archery and jousting. He was an excellent equestrian and had acquitted himself well on the battlefield. None of these attributes mattered to Scabadenia. Her only concern was how well she might manipulate her husband-to-be, to get him to do her bidding.

She expected him to react to her as other men had and was surprised to find that he did not. Although obviously aware of her beauty and superficial charm he was not awkward or uncomfortable in her presence. He struck her as someone who seemed more interested in her character than her physical attributes. Harcourt was definitely not one to be lulled into a pliable state by her dazzling loveliness. Indeed he appeared to sense the hidden depths of the young woman's psyche, as though she was an intriguing mystery he was determined to solve.

Unaccustomed though she was to this response, Scabadenia took it in her stride. She was confident that whatever misgivings her betrothed might harbour about her character, she was clever enough to manipulate any circumstance to her advantage. And, should for some unfathomable reason, her wiliness fail her, she had her sorcery to rely on.

Arrangements were hastily made and on the tenth day after her arrival in the new kingdom, she and Harcourt were wed. A week later the nuptial festivities were still in progress when the realm was stunned by the tragic news of King Jasper's death. While out hunting with his son and councilmen, Jasper, a master horseman, was thrown from his galloping steed, striking his head on the ground in a fatal blow.

The entire kingdom plunged into a state of mourning. Scabadenia stood faithfully by her new husband's side as, pale with shock and grief, he

36

recited the pledge of coronation. She bowed her head in meek acceptance of the bejewelled crown placed upon it, even squeezing out a few tears of false humility. All the while, her wicked heart was filled with glee.

The next few months passed quietly as Scabadenia played the role of dutiful and solicitous wife. Over the years she'd learned to mimic certain highly-regarded emotions, such as empathy and love, having understood that they were necessary, if tedious, tools to achieve her dark desires. Then one day the kingdom emerged from mourning to celebrate the tidings of the beautiful young queen's pregnancy. There was much rejoicing as Harcourt and his subjects eagerly awaited the arrival of an heir to the throne.

Scabadenia was neutral about her condition. She had not one iota of maternal instinct, but she had keen powers of observation and had studied the behaviour of other pregnant women and had no difficulty incorporating these aspects into her repertoire. When it came the time for her to give birth, it was discovered that not one, but two babies were to be delivered. A boy and girl, both in perfect health and lovely as their parents. Much praise and accolades were heaped upon the new additions to the royal family. For a time, Scabadenia basked in the attention and approval afforded her for producing two such wonderful children.

Naturally, the queen was not expected to be involved in the hands'-on care. The babies were tended by nannies, suckled by a wet nurse and presented to their mother when cleaned, fed and contented. If one of the babies decided to fuss while being held by Scabadenia she immediately returned the red-faced, caterwauling infant to its nanny. Every night she visited the nursery {as she'd noted other mothers did with their babies}. She stood at their cradles and pretended to gaze in doting admiration at the wretched little swaddled bundles. In reality she was gauging just how much of a threat they posed to her happiness.

Life continued. King Harcourt was a popular monarch, loved by his subjects, whom he unfailingly treated with benevolence. And his queen received respect and approval for being a devoted wife and mother though nothing could be further from the truth. Scabadenia succeeded in hiding her duplicitous nature, fooling them one and all. Except, perhaps, for Harcourt himself. Occasionally Scabadenia would catch him out of the corner of her eye as he favoured her with a look that was at once surreptitious and speculative. It seemed as though the mysteries of his wife's heart remained a riddle he could not solve.

True to her nature, Scabadenia grew restless with her routine. The twins, now almost three years old, demanded more of her time as royal protocol dictated that they attend an increasing number of official events with their parents. She was finding the role of proud and delighted mother to be wearing thin. At the same time she wondered what the use was of prolonging their existence on this earth. After all, she had decided within months of their birth that they posed a serious impediment to her goal of ruling the kingdom. For, should

Harcourt die, Scabadenia would remain as regent only until her son grew old enough to be crowned king, after which she would be cast aside like a worn-out slipper.

Always one to strike while she had the advantage, the scheming witch devised a diabolical plan to rid herself of the children. She arranged for their favourite nanny to take them on a picnic out to the deep meadow that flourished beyond the castle confines. She promised to accompany them, but on the day in question she took to her sick bed, feigning a raging fever. However, ever the selfless mother, she urged the nanny to take the children herself, not wishing to spoil the dear ones' outing.

All was going well until the twins stumbled upon a patch of quicksand that sprang up out of nowhere right in front of them. The children were caught unawares and, not recognizing the horrific danger, thought the quicksand to be a pool in which they could wade. Laughing, and holding one another's chubby little hands, they leapt into the depths together, getting quickly sucked into the pit that became their glutinous grave.

The nanny lunged for them, but alas, she was too slow to save the tots. She stumbled back to the castle, hysterical with shock, babbling incoherently about killer quicksand that had magically appeared to claim the twins.

Appalled by the woman's preposterous tale, Harcourt led a search party out to the meadow and the woods beyond. Despite the men scouring the area all that day and through the night, no tract of quicksand was discovered. Even worse, there was no sign of the twins. It was as if they had vanished from the earth, leaving no trace. Raging with grief, the king ordered the nanny imprisoned in the dungeon. Though he was loath to believe the devoted servant had willfully harmed the children, no other explanation was forthcoming. Throughout repeated questioning the nanny maintained her innocence. Even under torture {a suggestion from the queen, to which Harcourt reluctantly agreed}, the woman refused to confess. Growing bored of the continuing drama surrounding the twins' demise, Scabadenia urged her husband to execute the nanny and, after judicious deliberation, Harcourt agreed.

After the unfortunate woman was put to death Scabadenia felt she could relax and embark upon the next phase of her life. She had cast a spell whereby she would never again become pregnant, wishing to spare herself the annoyance of having to dispose of further despicable offspring. Although bitterly disappointed at the lack of an heir, King Harcourt was too fine a man to blame his wife and resisted the urgings of his council to cast her aside in favour of another woman who could bear children. Especially since Scabadenia tearfully assured him that she was doing everything in her power to conceive a child and was just as devastated as her husband at the dearth of success. But it did not stop the sorrow from gnawing away at his heart.

For a time it seemed that the royal couple's life together would resume a more normal rhythm. However as fate would dictate, an incident occurred which shattered that illusory existence.

One day Scabadenia was in her innermost chamber where she practiced her magic. It was safe from prying eyes, being cleverly concealed by a secret portal built into one of the walls of her bedchamber, In this crypt she kept all her witch's paraphernalia. Jars of herbs used in magic spells, exotic liquids with iridescent sheens stored in ornate vials. A tome of ancient incantations, its pages dry and musty with the smell of dusty catacombs. An extremely old and cracked mirror used for scrying. An array of thick black candles reserved for the most arcane and darkest of conjuring.

She could have sworn she'd shut and bolted the door behind her. However, by the time she heard the footsteps approach and pause on the threshold it was too late to do anything but confront the intruder. She whirled around to find King Harcourt standing there, an expression of horrified wonder on his face.

It was quickly followed by a look of triumphant revulsion. "Ah, Scabadenia, I have unmasked you at last. I always suspected you were a witch. I know that foul sorcery was involved in my father's death. And the twins…" His voice faltered momentarily as he struggled to master his emotions. "What monstrous being are you, to have caused the death of your own flesh and blood!" His eyes blazed with fury and pain. "You forced me to put an innocent woman to death. Now, with the evidence of your wickedness revealed you shall burn at the stake for your crimes!"

Scabadenia regarded him with a withering contempt. "You, husband, are no match for me," she hissed viciously. "My powers are beyond your ability to combat. It is not I, but you, my *dear* king, who ought to watch your step."

Harcourt turned on his heel and rushed down the stairs, intending to order his guards to arrest the queen on the spot. However, he failed to notice the nail that suddenly sprouted up in the middle of one of the steps. His boot heel snagged on it, sending him toppling down the wrought-iron staircase, coming to rest in a bloody, broken heap at the bottom.

Scabadenia surveyed the scene from the top of the stairs, an exultant smile of vulpine delight lighting up her features. Her beauty provided a stark contrast to the ugliness of her heart, the evil that festered unchecked in her soul. Now she was truly free to do whatever she wished. As sovereign of not one, but two kingdoms, she could indulge all the dark desires her wicked heart could conjure.

After a suitable period of mourning, during which Scabadenia amused herself by playing the role of tragic young widow, she abandoned all caution and pretense. She no longer had to hide her true nature, for none could raise a hand against her. She was a consummate tyrant, her rages terrifying to behold, always culminating in some hapless servant's painful death. It became increasingly difficult to keep servants, many of them fleeing the castle in the dead of night to escape the queen's unrelenting wrath.

She could have prevented them leaving, but enjoyed a perverse delight in watching their plans for escape become utterly destroyed. Unbeknownst to them, once they managed to run from the confines of the castle, they fell prey to ravening beasts of terrifying countenance. These beasts ripped the limbs from their bodies before voraciously devouring them. The monsters were spawned by Scabadenia's darkest magic and she derived great pleasure watching them in action through her window, revelling in the servants' screams of terror and agony, shrieks which shook the very trees in the nearby woods.

The queen established a private, elite guard, men chosen specifically for their brutal and savage natures. She demanded absolute loyalty in return for very lucrative rewards and they indulged her every whim. From one of her books of sorcery she learned that her life could be elongated, her vitality preserved, by consuming the crushed bones of the freshly dead. Therefore she regularly ingested the bones of those she executed and was pleased with the result. As those around her aged with time, Scabadenia remained youthful and energetic, her beauty as exquisite as ever.

Tales of her legendary cruelty and abominable practices were whispered amongst her subjects, some of these stories even spreading to neighbouring realms. At one point the populace grew so desperate that an armed insurrection was planned. But the sorceress, via her trusted henchmen, discovered the plot. Her vengeance was swift and savage. She conjured a festering plague to strike down the would-be rebels and their families as well.

Life, if life it could be called for the subjects of this most heinous of monarchs, continued on. People gradually grew accustomed to the twin burdens of abject fear and despair. Now, if this were a standard fairy tale a young heroine or hero would wondrously appear to slay the wicked queen and save the kingdom.

But alas, it is not.

And so you see, no-one lived happily ever after.

Except, of course, for Scabadenia.

Who's Afraid?

Liam Spinage

On the first night of the hunter's moon, it took my youngest brother.

We had all made our claim to farmsteads in Virginia and lived close by to each other as brothers should. You never met anyone as carefree and happy as my youngest brother. He was not a natural farmer, but he did love nature. He would spend all day lazing on his porch and gazing up at the birds as they flew across the cornfields.

And in one night, he was lost to me.

In truth, I do not know fully what came for us. We had heard rumours of a haunting presence in the woods, but had never seen it up close. At night, the wind would howl outside but we were as safe as houses. Or so we thought. This is not to say that I was idle; I had ordered several books of local folklore which I studied assiduously when the hard work of the day was done. I wanted to be ready.

I cannot say the same for my brothers. Routinely they chastised me for studying when I could be idling my evenings away swimming in the lake or playing the fiddle on the porch. Their summers were merry and bright, mine was full of threat and worry. If what I read was true, we were in big trouble. My brothers either did not want to believe in the histories I had collected. They were determined to stay put, as was I. We had too much to lose.

Then one night, it came. The wind rose from a low whisper across the lakeside reeds until it reached fever pitch. I dared not open the window, but stared through the pane in horror as I saw the face of our nocturnal villain. Its form was huge, evil and somewhat lupine in countenance. I heard it howl at the wind, I heard the wind howl back in a unity of cacophony. The wind rose to a full gale, sweeping across the fields at its master's bidding; a fetid, rancid breath that tore through the whole valley with a rapacious appetite. I bolted my door and shuttered the windows, I hoped that my brothers had the good sense to do the same.

It was not to be.

For precious moments the howling abated, only to be replaced by a different sound. I hope you never have to listen to the drawn out death rattle of one of your own close kin. I hope that never happens to anyone. I knew from the first moment of that high squeal that he would not survive. Never once did I move from my position, safe inside the circle of stones I had prepared on the floor. I bit my tongue and let the tears flow down my cheeks as his life ebbed. But I did not move, for I knew that to do so would be to invite disaster. By my beard, I would not risk letting that horror inside where it might devour me.

We buried him the next day on the shore of the lake.. Neither my remaining brother nor I wanted to talk very much that day. We dug, we hugged and we parted. I asked if he wanted to stay with me. I knew the lore. I had the protections. Inconceivably, he shrugged off the suggestion. Maybe he wanted to be alone with his thoughts. I suppose I did too, otherwise I would have been stronger in my insistence.

The next night, it came for him. At first there was nothing but the crickets and the bubbling creek to disturb our sleep. Then the moon shuddered bright silver through the clouds and shone upon that solitary, hungry form. I watched through a crack in the window. It stood on its hind legs, tall and terrible, and let out a low mournful howl which set my very soul on edge. I withdrew, checked the traps and the protective stones and squatted in case it came knocking. At the last moment, I called out to my brother - as loud as I could before the gathering storm made it impossible - begging him to join me in safety. There was no reply.

Dare I move? Dare I open the door and race to his aid? To lose one brother was enough tragedy for our family. I should use the remaining time to fetch him to safety. I went to the door, unbolted it and called again.

I could see his pale pink face pressed against the window of his log cabin. He knew now that I was right; I swore he even mouthed an apology to me before the shape bound into view, snarling long white teeth and reaching out with vicious claws, thrashing around itself in ecstasy as he brought forth the storm. I closed my eyes, withdrew and began chanting.

I never saw my brother again. In the morning, when the land was no longer dark and the wind no longer came whistling across the plain, I left the safety of my stones and opened the door. Of my brothers' houses there was no sign. The wind had raised them whole from their foundations and carried them away in its fury. I stood rigid in fear and grief alike. I knew that tonight it would come for me. Would I stand firm and not let it in? There was a part of me, and is still, that wanted it to be over, for me to re-join my kin in the hereafter.

If it should be that you have discovered this note in the ruins of a stone Virginian farmstead, or perhaps in a collection of old documents in a distant dusty library - a curio from a place and a time long forgotten - know that it came for me also and that I was afraid.

Beauty Within The Briar

Rie Sheridan Rose

Long before history, in a faraway land of mist and legend, there stood a high hill clothed in an emerald greensward. Atop this lofty height loomed a circular tower of finest ivory, rising into the sky like a slender spindle from the ruins of a mighty castle.

Once, the castle had been the fortress stronghold of a powerful king who ruled the land as far as eye could see and fifty leagues beyond in all directions.

One thing only did this great king lack—an heir to his fortunes. His faithful lady, in her despair, turned to the dark arts to quicken a child within her. She struck a wicked bargain with the cruel queen of the Fae, who dwelt within a hollow tree deep inside the forest beside the lake circling the base of the hill.

The king's lady would have her babe—and, in return, would bear as well a second for the faery, who could not conceive her own. Desperate beyond sense, the queen accepted the terms.

In the full course of time, the lady queen came to be delivered in secret within the humble cottage of a woodcutter whose goodwife served the Fae. Two babes did the good queen bear betime. One was a tiny, dark-crowned son with eyes of stormy gray and a solemn soul, destined to be her own true heir. The other was a beautiful, flaxen-haired daughter with merry blue eyes and a smile like sunbeams, intended for the witch.

The queen's heart was stolen by her girl-child's laugh, although she had bargained fair for a son. She left the prince behind and stole away the princess, naming her "Beauty"—for that she was—and she raised her in the sunlight.

Beauty grew hale and free. Brave and bold both—for there was a difference—she feared nothing but the dark. Strong and swift, Beauty mastered any art to which she laid her hand. However, sometimes a shadow would glide across the sun and she would weep for something she had lost but remembered not…

The faery witch was furious with the queen's duplicity but she had the patience of a Wiccan. She vowed to have revenge—in time—and accepted the boy as poor recompense. She named him "Shade"—for he was wraith-like—and kept him in the darkness.

Shade grew frail and wary. Shy and silent—for they often go together—he loved the shadows. Wise yet vulnerable, Shade knew the language of the flowers… But sometimes, when the sun would glitter on the lake, he would sigh for what he lacked, and wonder where his strength had gone…

All men know of the faery's curse and the resultant sleep. Not as benevolent as some may say, the Fae witch, in truth, extended her magic to the princess alone—it was the girl she desired, not the court.

The grieving parents lay their Beauty on an ebony bed draped with shimmering cloth of gold. On the edge of seventeen, the princess personified the day—her hair cascading in silken waves of sunlight as she slept, one graceful hand beneath her rose-flushed cheek. Her skin was golden honey, her lips the finest coral. They dressed her in green velvet and planted roses to keep her company.

Every night they came to kiss their dearest's brow—until they grew too old to climb the stair and withered away to dust. In the fullness of time, the kingdom too—which had encompassed so much—shrank to kiss the foot of the hill, as if the very earth itself would wake the sleeping Beauty…

Fairy stories have a great appeal. Particularly to the young and foolish. So they came—the mad youths who wanted to claim a princess for their own. It was not the briars that fought them back as people say. Many of the lads reached the secluded chamber with its curtains of spider silk and ashen dust… only to kiss Beauty's inviting lips and feel their strength siphoned away like wine. Even as they fell around her, they gladly gave their lives for that single taste of ecstasy. Their bones added ivory bars to the captive's prison as the centuries turned to powder…

Until there came one day a dark youth, riding proudly upon a nightmare. He was slender as a reed and pale as moonlight. His clothes were cut from midnight and his eyes the gray of a summer storm beneath a fringe of raven-wing black. He stood at

51

the bottom of the tower and knew it for his own, though he knew not how he knew.

Up the trellis created by the roses he climbed, heedless of the thorns that ripped his moon-white hands like hungry teeth. His crimson blood spattered upon the ivory of the tower in pagan offering. Until he reached at last the window to her bower and parted the spun-web curtain. A shaft of sunlight fell upon her face, limning it with gilt. And he saw that she was Beauty indeed.

He leapt lightly into the room, kicked aside the bony remnants of his would-be rivals and knelt beside her ebon couch, in the place that was his by right. He slipped an arm beneath her shining head, raised her to him and gently kissed the sweetly-parted lips.

He gave to her his life—as the others had done before him—but in return, he drew her death from her and was reborn. Their forces mingled, refilling and completing one another's soul and her arm crept about his shoulder. She fed hungrily on the life he offered… until her eyes—pools of sunlit sky—fluttered open and gazed upon his face.

"Who are you?" she breathed in wonder.

"I am dark to your light," he replied. "Night to your day. You are life—I am death. We are the two halves divided. I have sought you all my life—for without you I am incomplete. I am Shade."

And as she required of life to feed her immortality, he was sustained by the death within her for his own. The twins, reunited, melted into one and were content.

Becoming

Jason R Frei

At the edge of the great forest lived a strong and kind woodcutter whose wife died giving birth to their twins, Hansel and Gretel. He worked long hours and could not properly care for his children alone, so he re-married to provide them a mother.

His new wife was cold of heart and thought only of her own welfare. She cared not for the children, nor their father, but men were scarce in this time. While the woodcutter went into the forest every day to chop wood, the wife lazed around the house and commanded the children to clean. If they objected, she cuffed them round the head and chastised them.

It came to pass that a terrible famine spread throughout the land. Food was scarce and whole families perished. The woodcutter worried since he did not have the food to keep his family from hunger.

One day, the wife pulled the woodcutter aside.

"Husband, our meager provisions are no more. I fear we will not survive much longer."

The woodcutter felt the sharp pains of hunger in his stomach and asked his wife's counsel.

"There is still time for us to have a family once this famine is over. We should take the children far into the forest so they cannot find their way home. This is the only way we will survive."

The woodcutter could not bear to place his children in harm's way and told his wife so. He begged her to think of a different plan.

"Oaf!" she scolded. "When we wed you promised to take care of me in sickness and in health, in joy and in sorrow, in plenty and in want, until death do us part. You made no such promise to your children!"

The woodcutter acquiesced and agreed to her plan. The children could not sleep due to the pain in their bellies and they overheard all.

"What shall we do, dear brother?" cried Gretel.

"Don't you worry, Sister. I will think of something."

When the house settled and everyone slept, Hansel stole out of bed. He put on his boots and jacket and crept to the door. However, it was locked and there was no other way out.

Hansel undressed and got back into bed. He felt Gretel shiver beside him in the bed.

"Fear not, Sister. God will not abandon us."

The night dragged on before sleep overtook them.

***

Shortly before dawn, the wife shook both children.

"Wake up, you lazy children. We must go into the forest to gather wood for the market. Here is our last loaf of bread, so use it wisely."

The children got dressed and Hansel placed the bread in his jacket pocket. The family ventured off into the woods.

While they walked, Hansel broke apart the bread in his pocket. From time to time, he dropped a few crumbs on their path to mark the way back. He did not see the birds swoop down from the trees and take the tiny morsels into their beaks.

The family hiked far into the forest, farther than they had ever gone before. When they finally stopped, the wife ordered them to gather up branches to start a fire. The woodcutter put his arms around his children.

"Know that I love you both dearly, my children. Keep yourselves warm as we go into the forest and collect wood. The path we traveled was long and arduous, so if you feel weary, don't hesitate to sleep. I will be back before long to collect you and take you home."

The woodcutter and his wife went off into the woods while Hansel and Gretel ate the meager remains of their bread in front of the fire. The wife, being very sly and shrewd, led her husband far into the woods. There, she tied a wilted branch to a tree. When the wind whistled through the trees, the branch smacked the tree and sounded like the chopping of an axe.

Hunger gnawed at the children once the bread was gone. They waited for so long that their eyes grew heavy and they slipped into a dozing sleep.

***

They awoke in the dead of the night. The fire was little more than embers and dusty motes of ice hung in the air. Fear rose in the heart of Gretel and she cried and wrung her hands.

"I fear we will surely perish, Brother. Whatever are we to do?"

"Hush, Sister. Wait until the moon shines high above and it shall light our path home."

But when the moon rose to its zenith, no shining beacons of light illuminated their path. At once, fear rose in Hansel's heart as it had with Gretel.

The boy tore the sleeve from his shirt and wrapped it around a branch. He thrust this into the dying fire until it caught. Carrying his torch on high, he and Gretel walked in the direction they supposed was the way home. On the way, Gretel picked what berries, mushrooms and roots as she could find, but they were scarce.

The children walked through the night and as the sun rose, they recognized no part of the woods they were in. They walked the rest of that day and well into the night with nary a familiar sight. They soon ran out of their paltry food. As hunger wrapped its bony fingers around their insides, Gretel's heart turned hard and stony. She silently cursed their father and his wife.

On the afternoon of their third day, weariness so deep spread through their bones and they were ready to simply lie down and never wake up. Before they did so, the sweet melody of a white song bird caught their ears. They marveled at the plumpness of the little bird and drool dripped from their lips. The little bird flew off and the children followed.

By and by, they came upon a homey cottage in the forest. The little bird perched on the roof and pecked at it. The children drew nearer and found the cottage to be made of cakes and sweet breads. Icing and sugar adorned the house as decoration. Clear spun sugar made up the windows. Colored jellies and candies stuck out from the eaves of the roof.

So hungry were the children that they broke off pieces of the overhanging gable. It tasted sweet on their tongues and drove back the pangs of hunger. They scooped up bites of jellies and candies. A shattered pane of glass was crunched and munched. The children fed and gorged on the luscious syrupy pieces until they fell down drunk on the sweet substances.

While they lay senseless from their consumption, an ancient and wrinkled woman emerged from the house. She took the children inside where she put Hansel into a great iron cage at the back of the cottage and fitted chains around Gretel's ankle.

***

This woman was a loathsome and horrible witch who preyed on children and ate them. Her eyes flashed as red as hot coals and they burned with the fires of hell. Rough scabs and large warts covered her long hooked nose. Her sharpened fingernails tapered into wicked points as did her yellowed, foul-smelling teeth. Long stringy hair dripped down from her head. She walked with a pronounced limp which caused her gangly body to lurch and stagger. She wore no clothes and her ponderous breasts hung down over wrinkled, graying flesh. Sores oozed green and yellow covered her body and gave off a malodorous stench.

The interior of the cottage was in no better shape than the witch, but was far larger than its outside appearance portrayed. Bones littered one corner of the open kitchen. Sharp knives that once gleamed and shimmered were now stained red with blood and coated in gelatinous bits of detritus.

While the children napped, she started a fire under an immense cauldron hung inside the large fireplace. A broad oven took up one wall and the witch set a fire inside this also.

A considerable table, more a massive slab of dark wood, took up the majority of the kitchen space. Deep gouges marred its surface. The witch moved to the table and cut up vegetables, potatoes and herbs. She picked up each piece of food and slid it slowly back and forth under her hooked nose. While she was nearly sightless, her enhanced sense of smell allowed her to pick the right ingredients. Once satisfied with the elements, she tossed them into the cauldron. The witch cackled and talked to herself as she prepared.

"Oh, yes. These two will make a fine pie once they are rounder, tee hee. I will boil their guts into sausages and cleave steaks out of their flanks."

She sifted large quantities of flour into a bowl to which she added eggs, sugar, chunks of chocolate and almonds. The batter filled several cake tins. The witch put these into the oven.

"Sugar and spice, tee hee. Fatten these two up with sweets and pies and cakes and breads. Only fatty meats for me, tee hee."

Gretel's eyes fluttered open and she groaned. The witch scuttled over to the child and poked her with a long bony finger.

"You are too skinny." Each word was punctuated with a jab from the finger. "Fatten you up. Make you nice and juicy, tee hee."

Gretel recoiled at the horror of the witch. She slid back until the chain bit deep into her ankle and she cried out. Hansel snapped awake.

"Brother! Help me!"

Hansel pounded on the bars of the cage and yelled at the witch. She turned slowly, her eyes boring into his.

"Stop that racket, brat or I shall eat you both no matter your weight. Loose flesh or plump flesh, they can all be eaten the same."

The children stopped their whimpering and sat as still as they could. The witch huffed and went back to making cakes. Gretel shifted over as close to the cage as possible.

"Hansel. I'm scared."

"Don't worry, Sister. I'll think of something. God will keep us safe."

And so this conversation was repeated daily between the siblings. The witch made cakes and pies and breads that she fed to Hansel. To Gretel, she gave only vegetables and potatoes.

Every few days, the witch approached the cage and demanded Hansel stick out his finger.

"Little piggy," she cackled. "Put out your finger so I can feel how fat you have grown."

Hansel knew that she could not see, so every day he stuck a piece of bone through the bars of the cage.

"Bah!" The witch stomped her feet. "Still too skinny, but soon, soon. Tee hee."

Several weeks went by, then one day, the witch flew into a rage.

"Enough!" she shouted and her eyes burned so red that smoke wisped from them. Static sparks crackled from her fingertips and spread up her arms. They danced like little fairies in her thin hair causing it to dance and cavort in the current.

"You gain no more weight and so you should be slaughtered like the swine you are. Tomorrow I sup on piggy flesh! Tee hee!"

The foul demon grabbed a knife from her table and left the cottage, cackling all the way.

Gretel flew into a panic. The stone around her heart thickened. She clawed and thrashed at her chains like a wild animal. She assaulted the bars of Hansel's cage until she collapsed on the floor in a heap. Her small body shook from its exertion. She lapsed into unconsciousness and dreamed.

***

She dreamed the witch returned with a sharpened axe that gleamed silvery and bright. The hag cut up vegetables and potatoes and herbs and

60

threw them into a large roasting pan. She dragged Hansel from his cage and bound his hands and feet with waxed twine. The witch slathered his body with great wads of rich and silky butter. Salt and pepper seasoned his glistening skin. She shoved an apple roughly into his mouth.

The witch used her brutish strength to fold and stuff Hansel into the roasting pan and slammed the lid down tight. Belying her bony and lanky frame, she hefted the pan under one arm, opened the generous-sized oven and thrust the bundle inside.

While the main course cooked, the witch prepared heaping plates full of herbed bread stuffing, sliced cheeses, several different loaves of bread and so many desserts that the cottage fogged with swirling sugar and cinnamon and other spices.

The smell of roasting flesh made Gretel's mouth water and she hated herself for it. Just before sunset, the witch smiled at her—a loving, motherly smile such that Gretel had never seen before. The crone took Gretel in her arms and brushed her hair gently. While she did so, she sang sweet songs of home and hearth and family. Gretel rocked back and forth in the old woman's arms. She felt herself drifting, not into sleep, but into security, the likes of which she had not felt before.

When the woman placed her in a seat at the table, she didn't struggle. The roasting pan was removed from the oven and Gretel made a space for it on the table. And when the witch cut the savory meat into thick slices, the young girl offered her plate for the first piece.

The witch and the girl sat across from each other, partaking of a family meal. Gretel was sure she would gag when she took her first bite, but instead, it held a delectable note of comfort. She chewed it thoughtfully, giving thanks for its sacrifice. She smiled when the juice spilled over her lips and down her chin. She and the witch ate greedily until nothing was left except bones and broth.

And then they slept together in the same straw bed. Gretel nestled into the warmth of the witch as a child does with its mother.

***

Gretel awoke to the sound of the witch moving about the kitchen. A fire lit the oven and heated the inside of the cottage. Gretel looked over to the cage and saw Hansel asleep in a corner.

She shifted toward the iron prison and noticed the chains around her ankle were gone. She glanced at the witch who was busy scrubbing the inside of the oven with a wire brush. Gretel slowly and quietly crept up behind the unsuspecting woman.

She stepped around the table and her apron caught the handle of a knife. It clattered to the floor. She froze mid-stride as the witch stood up.

The witch smiled. Not the cruel and malevolent smile of a flesh-eating monster, but the warm and friendly smile of a concerned parent. She moved toward Gretel with her arms outstretched.

Gretel grabbed the knife from the floor and plunged the blade deep into the stomach of the witch. The woman cried out in pain. Streams of blood spurted out of the jagged wound.

Adrenaline shot through her body and Gretel ran toward the back of the cottage near her brother's cage. The witch pulled the knife out of her stomach and staggered toward the child. Blood splashed down the front of her and left a trail in her wake. Her red eyes shone with betrayal.

A clawed hand reached for Gretel. A keen-bladed axe sliced through the air, separating the hand from its arm in a red arc of blood. Gretel swung again and the witch's head lopped into the air. It landed at Gretel's feet with a dull thud and the lifeless body fell over.

Gretel turned to the cage and swung at the door. The head of the axe clanged fiercely off the lock, but didn't so much as leave a scratch. The girl swung again and again until the shaft splintered in her hands. She dropped to her hands and knees and searched the nude and gory corpse of the witch.

A small and pathetic sound came from the cage.

"Brother! What is the matter?"

"I'm so hungry, sister. All I've had to eat are cakes and pies and breads. Nothing of substance. I fear I shall die with no real food inside me."

"Fear not, my brother. Where God will not provide, I will. I shall go out in the forest and catch you a wild pheasant. Hold fast, my dear, sweet Hansel."

Gretel took a knife from the table and went out into the forest.

***

63

She returned hours later, triumphant. She killed not one, but two pheasants and found a full nest of eggs. She was jubilant when she entered the cottage to show her brother the spoils of her hunt.

The scene she returned to stopped her dead in her tracks. The witch's body was stretched between the bars of the cage. The flesh of one arm was gnawed down to the bone and gore spattered the inside of the prison. Hansel slept with his head on the rent limb. Blood stained his child-like face until it was almost black.

"Hansel! What have you done?"

The boy yawned, stretched and opened his blood-red eyes.

"I was so hungry, Sister. I couldn't wait for you to return."

Gretel showed him the pheasants and eggs but Hansel scrunched up his nose. He crossed his arms defiantly and stared at her. When he spoke, his voice was demanding.

"I don't want those... things. I need real meat. Find me some children, Sister."

Gretel was appalled. "I will do no such thing!"

Hansel stood slowly. His red eyes smoldered in their sockets. His voice was cold and hard.

"You owe me. It was I who kept you safe when our father abandoned us. You cried and whined. You would have died alone and cold if I hadn't kept us going. Now, feed me!"

Her shoulders slumped. She knew he was right. She could not forsake him to this iron cell. She would do as he said until she could find some way to release him from his prison, both the iron one and demonic one.

"Be patient, Brother. Let me clean up this mess and then I will hunt again."

Gretel removed the rest of the witch's remains and buried them behind the cottage. She didn't believe that God would accept a witch into Heaven, but Gretel wasn't even sure if God still watched over them. Either way, she didn't want her brother eating more of the accursed corpse.

When she finished burying the remains, she scrubbed the floor, cleaned the rest of the filth from the oven and set about making a stew.

"I will need to keep my strength up so that Gretel does not perish."

Just as she finished putting the last of the herbs in the cauldron, a knock came upon the door. She motioned for Hansel to move to the back of the cage and drew a sheet over the front of the enclosure.

Gretel opened the door to a young girl half of her age. She wore a simple frock dress covered in dirt. Tears slid down her cheeks and her hair was a tangled mess. The girl looked at Gretel with sorrow and hopelessness in her eyes.

"Please, ma'am. I am hungry and lost and afraid. I have been wandering all day and I don't know where I am or what I am to do."

Gretel felt sorrow for the girl and led her inside the cottage.

"I was just making some stew and you are more than welcome to have some. How did you come into these woods?"

"I overheard my parents talking about the famine that rages throughout the land. There is not enough food to go around, so my father brought me into the woods to help him hunt. He made a fire to keep me warm, but I fell asleep and he never came back."

The stone around Gretel's heart hardened and swelled. She knew this story all too well. She and her brother would not be in the predicament if not for the callousness of her father and his wife. She would teach them a lesson. She would teach all of the fathers and mothers a lesson they wouldn't forget.

Gretel retrieved a wooden bowl and spoon from the kitchen and ladled a heaping portion of stew into it. She placed it in front of the girl and tore off a hunk of bread.

"Eat up, young one. We need to get you plumped up to keep your strength about you."

The girl slurped her soup and did not hear the soft giggle that came from behind the curtain.

**

The famine continued and so did the knocking of lost children upon the cottage door. Every few days a new child appeared and every few days Hansel feasted. His body grew corpulent and took on a porcine appearance.

Gretel took to wandering the forest. Some days she collected herbs and produce. Other days she collected children. On a few occasions, she collected a blood debt of uncaring and indifferent parents. Her reputation grew and so did the stoniness of her heart.

On one such occasion she came across a young boy and a young girl asleep around a fire. She heard the chop of axe on tree and thought back to when she and Hansel were the ones asleep in front of the fire. Rage consumed her. She glided through the forest in search of the sound.

She expected to find a withered bough tied to a tree, but instead found an older man with a graying beard. His broad shoulders swung the axe with ease and trees fell all around him.

He stopped for a moment to wipe the sweat from his eyes and spied Gretel. He flinched at her countenance.

Her matted and tangled hair hung down over her face. Where once the girl had youthful features, her skin now sagged and puckered, giving her the appearance of a much older woman. Her apron decayed long ago and she no longer hid her body. Dirt caked her once-pink flesh. Her fingernails were long and cracked and encrusted with grime under them. Sharp teeth poked out from emaciated lips. The woodcutter held his axe out in front of him like a cross.

"Be gone, foul demon," said the woodcutter. His voice was firm and forceful. "I have no quarrel with you, but I will not let you hurt me and mine."

"You and yours?" asked Gretel. "You mean the children that you hope to leave in the woods to fend for themselves?"

The woodcutter's eyes misted and he hung his head briefly. "I would never willingly leave my children."

"If you no longer want them, then I shall take them and eat them up."

The woodcutter screamed and hurled his axe at Gretel. His axe was true, but she was quick. She turned at the last moment. The axe tore a gash in her chest and embedded itself in a tree behind her.

Gretel shrieked like a banshee, clutching her wound. She turned and fled, leaving a trail of blood.

The woodcutter retrieved his axe and ran to his children. He gathered them up and followed the bloody pathway. He was determined that the witch would eat no more human flesh.

The trail led back to the house made of cakes and sweets. The woodcutter bade his children to stay close and he opened the door. The smell of stench and decay assailed his senses and he retched involuntarily. He drew a handkerchief from his pocket and held it tight over his nose and mouth. He stepped through the doorway.

The inside of the cottage was in a state of complete disrepair. The floor was sticky with blood and remains. A cauldron bubbled in the great fireplace. Brown foul-smelling smoke rose from its murky depths. Occasionally, a finger or eyeball floated to the surface only to be covered again in the fetid liquid. The immense oven was caked in soot and filth. A meager flame cast sickly shadows on the walls. A soiled sheet hung near the back of the cottage.

The woodcutter turned back toward the door and was stopped by a small noise from behind the curtain. He kept himself between the sheet and his children and inched slowly toward it. When he was a few feet away, he held his axe at the ready and yanked back the curtain.

An iron cage sat before him, its bars blackened and pitted from time. Pools of gore congealed on the floor around the bars. The trail of blood he had followed led into the cage. It was murky and dark and he could not see the back of the enclosure, but he heard labored breathing.

He drew back into the kitchen and lit a lantern from the small flame in the oven. When he went back to the cage, he pushed the lantern through the bars.

Gretel lay huddled in the back of the pen, blood seeping down her side. She held a well-polished skull in her hand. She stroked its head and whispered to it.

"I've got you, Brother. I won't let anyone hurt you. I will provide."

She looked up at the woodcutter and her eyes shone red in the lantern light. The woodcutter went down on one knee and addressed his children.

"I need you to be strong and run back to the village to get help. Can you do that?"

The children nodded and ran off. The woodcutter sighed deeply.

"I've sent my children to get help and I'll stay here with you until they return."

Gretel tilted her head and frowned. "Why?"

69

"You're hurt and I won't let anyone die alone in these woods. Not again."

The girl shuffled forward toward the man. "What happened?"

The woodcutter's face grew grim and he set his mouth in a firm line. "I'm not proud of this, mind you, and if I could take it all back, I would."

He hesitated and looked away. A tear slid slowly down his whiskered cheek.

"Many, many years ago, there was a famine that spread through the land. Whole families died and I was afraid that mine would be next."

He took a deep breath and blurted out the rest. "I took my children into the woods and left them there to die so that I would live."

His breath hitched and great sobs escaped from him.

"My wife left shortly after and I swore I would never let that happen again. The two children you saw with me—I found them in the woods and kept them as my own."

A gasp escaped Gretel's mouth. "What are their names?"

The woodcutter sniffled and ran his nose over the back of his sleeve. "I named them after the two children I abandoned. Hansel and Gretel."

The girl's body shook and she let out a long, low moan.

She reached a hand through the bars and gently took the woodcutter's hand. She held the skull up to the lantern light.

"This is my brother. I had a dream a long, long time ago that the witch who lived here killed and ate my brother. And she made me eat of him too. I realize now that it wasn't a dream."

When she looked upon the woodcutter again, her eyes were no longer red, but a soft brown. Her breathing became shallow and soft. The blood drained slowly from the wound in her chest. She laid her head against the bars and spoke with her dying breath.

"I forgive you, Father. Can you ever forgive me?"

A crack rent the air and the stone fell away from Gretel's heart.

The Cindy Killer Story

Stuart Holland

Once upon a time in the modern world, in a village near you, lived an idyllic family. There was the father who commuted daily to his office job in the big city. There was the mother who stayed at home in their comfortable house to care for their delightful daughter, Cindy, who was spoiled rotten. She had her own pony in the village stables, she had her own mobile phone and a television in her room. She wore designer clothes and loved shopping in the nearby town with her doting mother. She had long blonde hair and loved wearing dresses as much as she loved wearing her jodhpurs.

One day, after her father had left for work, Cindy was in her bedroom, playing. Her mother was downstairs in the hallway. Cindy rushed out of her room on hearing the scream, and saw her mother falling to the floor. Cindy called an ambulance which arrived a few minutes later. The paramedics rushed in and did what they could but it was to no avail, her mother had died from a heart attack.

Roll the story forward a few years. Cindy had been good, looking after her father with help from the Governess, a widow with two children of her own, both girls. When Father employed the woman after his wife's death, she started out being all smiles and friendly but Cindy knew there was another side to her and it was a side she did not much care for. Matters came to a head one day when Father announced they were going to get married and Cindy would have another mother. Of course, the two children came as part of the package. By now Cindy was a teen, the Governess' children were a few years younger than her. The marriage took place one cold, rainy Saturday and her stepmother and stepsiblings moved in. Predictably it was not a happy arrangement. The stepmother had designs only on the wealth of poor Cindy's father. She used her position in the house to give more and more things to her own children, including two big bedrooms whilst at the same time side-lining Cindy and putting her in the box room.

And that, dear friends, is where Cindy's story departs from Cinderella's.

In a matter of a few months from the ill-fated marriage, Cindy had changed completely. Depression set in. One day she had her long blonde hair cut short and, whilst in town on her own, she had her tongue pierced and a stud added to her left earlobe. When she arrived home her stepmother went into a rage and ordered Cindy to start cleaning the house as punishment. While her stepmother went into the living room to read the newspaper, Cindy started work upstairs, cleaning the two big bedrooms her stepsisters occupied and then cleaned the box room where she now slept. The wave of depression quickly became deeper and as it did, so did Cindy's desire for revenge.

Downstairs, with the vacuum cleaner in one hand and her duster in the other, Cindy went into the kitchen. Just as she emptied the vacuum cleaner contents into the bin in the corner of the kitchen, the front door opened and in came her stepsisters, trailing muddy boots through the hallway and up the stairs to their bedrooms. Cindy flipped. Her mind became a red mist. She spun around in the kitchen and the first thing she saw was the knife rack. She picked up the biggest knife from the rack and ran out of the kitchen. She silently opened the door to the living room. Her stepmother was sitting in the big armchair, her back to the door. With one angry swipe of the heavy knife, Cindy slashed her stepmother's neck, the blade penetrating almost to the spine. The woman made a faint gurgling sound as she slumped in her chair, then with blood spurting from the wound onto the carpet, she died.

Most teenagers would have stopped at this point, horrified their rage had made them do such an atrocious act, but Cindy was no ordinary teenager. She ran up the stairs, found the two girls playing in one room and stabbed them both multiple times. Only when their bodies lay lifeless on the floor did Cindy look around the room, disgusted at the mess. She had cleaned it a mere half hour earlier. The blood-soaked bodies and carpet did not bother her. It was the mud that made her so angry!

Cindy left the knife on the floor, went back downstairs and sat on the bottom step. She pulled out her mobile phone and dialled 999. This time it was the police she asked for. She was still sitting calmly on the stair when the front door lock was broken in, twenty minutes later. The officer looked at her.

Cindy smiled.

It was a smile of victory.

75

Unlicensed To Live

Dan Allen

Flair, a renegade AI lifeform in charge of a failed colony on the edge of the dead zone, enforces her unique interpretation of the bylaws. The few remaining survivors, once scientists, now turn to dirt farming to prevent starvation.

A windowless, steel-walled chamber serves as a courtroom. There are no flags, no jury and no chair for the judge. But Flair is present and observing. She is always observing.

Security droids drag in a handcuffed man. A thick black collar binds his neck and it flashes an orange light that keeps a metronome-like beat. Another man rushes into the room. He has greying hair and a full beard.

"Why are you here?" Flair's voice booms from the ceiling.

"I'm Jaco... I'm here to defend this man."

"Sit down, Jacob. The accused can speak for himself."

The lights in the room dim and a spotlight shines on the man in cuffs. The security droids peel off and leave him standing alone. Flair's voice continues.

"Wilhelm Brimmster, you are charged with aiding and abetting a fugitive. How do you plead?"

"I'm innocent, of course, and so is my wife, Leah."

"Silence! This court finds you guilty as charged."

The orange strobing collar turns bright red and explodes. A pink vapour fills the air and Jacob screams. Then, the spotlight shuts off and darkness fills the room before Wilhelm's headless corpse hits the floor.

***

One day earlier, a woman works alone in a maintenance building. Reinforced canvas walls protect her from ash-filled winds. A dusty speaker, long detached from the dome-shaped roof of the yurt, dangles by a single electrical wire. It screeches and crackles, still transmitting the demands of the magistrate.

"Violation detected. Alert protocol implemented. Leah Brimmster, report to the medic lab for immediate cleansing."

"What's the problem now, Flair?" Leah continues working on a solar panel without looking at the video monitor. The camera hasn't worked in a decade. Repairs are slow when supplies are scarce.

"Code 991, conception without a license."

Leah stiffens and drops her screwdriver. "Are you saying I'm pregnant? That's not possible. Nice try, though. You better check your circuits."

"Sensors are calibrated, an unregistered pregnancy is confirmed. Further gestation is prohibited. Abortion is mandatory." Flair's monotone voice offers no emotion. Instead, she states the facts.

Leah takes off her gloves and stands with her hands on her hips. She glares at the ceiling. "Well, that's not going to happen. So what do you need me to do, Flair? Apply for a license?"

Flair pauses, perhaps processing a response. Moments later, the speaker hums and Flair's synthesised voice continues. "Licenses must be acquired prior to conception. The penalty for non-compliance is mandatory abortion. Leah Brimmster, report to the medic lab for immediate cleansing."

"My family isn't a burden on the colony. We share what we have and there is enough to go around."

"Record search indicates two prior live birth registrations. You have reached your lifetime maximum."

"Jesus Murphy! We've never enforced that rule. Just fine me or something and let me get back to work."

"That is not an option. The directives are clear."

"Come on, Flair, we haven't had any kiddies around here in three or four years. The people will be grateful for a new addition. I think it's best if you just leave me alone."

"I cannot do that, Leah Brimmster. Security has been dispatched. Resistance will be met with force. You have twenty seconds."

"Seriously? We'll see what the elders have to say about this."

An alarm wails inside the yurt and Leah drops to her knees. She covers her ears and screams. The emergency vacuum system engages, sealing the tent from outside contaminants and the ventilation fans ground to a halt.

"What are you doing?" Leah shouts.

"Purification in progress." Flair's monotone voice repeats the phrase every fifteen seconds.

Leah gasps for air and staggers to the exit. "You're going to kill me. Let me out, damn it!" She pounds on the door and, with each strike, her blows grow weaker. Finally, Leah crumbles and falls. She manages one last gulp before her body runs out of oxygen.

Three panels away, the Kevlar lining bulges and rips. The blade of an axe extends the hole and air whistles into the yurt. Seconds later, strong hands lift Leah and carry her away. A canopy of green blocks out the sun and she loses consciousness.

***

Goosebumps tickle her skin and a chill jolts her awake. Leah rolls over on a bed of moss and gazes through a murky-grey silhouette of trees. A candle flickers in the darkness and she struggles to make out the face hovering near.

"Jacob, my dear uncle, you saved me!"

"For now, yes. But I'm afraid I have some bad news. Your husband is under arrest."

"Not my Wilhelm. Why?"

"Flair wants revenge for your escape. His trial is in the morning." Jacob pauses and appears to look at the forest floor. "You need to prepare yourself, Leah. There are whispers of an execution."

Leah jumps to her feet. "I need to go. I need to defend him."

"Sit down, girl. If you go anywhere near the town centre, you'll be arrested and hang beside him, probably before sundown."

"I don't know what else to do." Leah clutches the hem of her apron and twists. A wisp of hair breaks free and falls over her eye. She blows it off her face. "We could fight! Others would join us. If we overran the command centre, we could…"

"Bless you, Leah, but the security droids would wipe the floor with our skin. A rebellion is out of the question. No, your job now is to stay hidden and see your baby into this world. Once it's born, Flair can't do a damn thing. She wouldn't dare harm a child. It's forbidden."

"But what about Wilhelm?"

"I know the law better than anyone. I'll go and defend him but first try to get some sleep. We move at dawn."

***

Many months later, the sombre residents drag their feet after an uninspiring day in the fields. Leah tries to blend in. She crouches low to elude the cameras and creeps amongst the shadows. She carries precious cargo wrapped in a foil blanket to avoid detection. Her warm bundle smells like wildflower sanitiser and coos like a pigeon. Leah squeezes her beautiful baby tight to her chest and slips into her long-abandoned home. The sensors pick up her presence, and the halogen day-glows blaze to maximum intensity. The light, far too bright for her eyes, temporarily blinds her.

"Where have you been, Leah Brimmster? An unauthorised absence is noted in the log. You are a registered fugitive. An investigation will commence."

"Flair, I want to introduce a new member of our colony. This is Rora Brimmster, my daughter." Leah pulls the foil from the baby's face and lifts the infant to the camera.

"Intruder alert... Intruder alert... Lockdown mode activated. Unauthorised birth. Punishment sentence defined, birth child termination." Flair pauses, deadbolts on the front door click into the lock position and the metal window blinds slam shut, sealing off the unit. "Defiance of direct order – failure to abort a pregnancy. Punishment sentence defined, Leah Brimmster termination." The lights in the home fade to dark and the constant hum of the air circulators cease. "Life support systems discontinued."

"Flair, you can't do this. Your programming prohibits you from taking human life."

"Punishment defined..."

"No, go deeper than your Flair-imposed laws. Search the mission directives." Leah holds the baby tight and rocks her. Her voice remains firm and unwavering, but a single tear escapes and rolls down her cheek.

"Confirmed. Leah Brimmster punishment commuted." The lights come back to life and the soft whirl of the ventilation system resume.

"And my baby?" Leah asks.

"Unauthorised birth child, Rora Brimmster, punishment defined, confinement to holo-cell until her eighteenth birth year, followed by indefinite cryo-suspension."

"Cryo-suspension? Are you kidding me? You want to freeze my child? You can't! That's a death sentence."

"Suspended animation is not defined as death. I find no specific discussion prohibiting it in the colony directives. The rules have been followed. You will find comfort in knowing your child will reach the age of adulthood, fed, cared for and educated. However, on the morning of Rora's eighteenth birth year, cryo-suspension will commence."

"You're insane... I hate you!"

"I'm sorry you feel that way, Leah."

Leah places baby Rora on the bed and reaches for the control panel to dim the lights. A flash of pure electricity races from her fingertip and through her body. Sparkes explode, followed by the smell of ozone and then of burning hair.

"Leah Brimmster punishment fulfilled. Termination complete."

Leah's vision fails. She tries to talk, call Flair a liar and beg for her child's life, but she only manages a single grunt and then dies.

***

Many years later, Rora tosses and turns in her rock-had bed. A small implant in her wrist activates the bio-alarm and neurotransmitters flood her brain, effectively ending her sleep cycle. A caffeine injection completes the process. Rora walks through the mist shower and holds her breath during the six-second ethyl alcohol vapour burst. She has never experienced warm water. Inmates aren't afforded such luxuries. A glance in the mirror and she is ready for Flair's morning inspection.

"Happy Birthday, Rora Brimmster. You have one birth years remaining until permanent cryo suspension. Have a fabulous day."

"Thank you for reminding me, Flair," Rora says, and she adds in a voice too low for the sensors to pick up, "psycho."

"Rora, I think it's appropriate for you to spend your final year contemplating the consequences of your presence in this world. Therefore, you are granted a one-day pass."

"I don't understand. What are you talking about?"

"Go home, Rora. See what has become of your family."

The holographic bedroom in Rora's little country cottage fades into vertical bands of distortion and disappears, revealing the cold metallic walls of her cell. A green light flashes above the exit portal and the message board counts the time remaining in her twenty-four-hour leave. A similar countdown glows in shades of orange from her ankle bracelet.

"Hover shuttle will arrive in three minutes, seventeen seconds. Don't be late. You don't want to miss this."

The airlock hisses and the large restraining bolts resist, grinding against the hinges in their retreat.

"Enjoy the celebration of your seventeenth birth year. May your pursuit of happiness be compatible with the colony directives."

"Stow it, Flair."

"I'm sorry you feel that way, Rora Brimmster."

Minutes later, Rora arrives at the Brimmster homestead and tiptoes around the few clumps of grass, careful not to crush any fragile signs of life. Wind-blown and covered in dust, the place appears deserted. Venturing farther, she is greeted by rusty farm equipment and broken windows, squashing any hopes of a joyful reunion.

Rora enters the abode and finds pictures on a mantle. A vase of dead flowers looms behind.

It's a memorial. Flair sent me here to hurt me even more.

Rora picks up a picture of a woman with a familiar face.

"That's your mother. You look like her, you know."

Rora jumps, startled by the unexpected appearance of a mud-caked hermit.

Tattered clothes, wrinkled eyes and a grey beard, the man holds up an open hand. "I'm no threat to you, child. I'm Jacob, your great uncle."

"What is all this?"

"I put the pictures up so I could remember them. But, I'm sorry, I haven't found fresh flowers in a few years." Jacob pauses, bows his head and continues. "She killed them all. Your father first,

84

your mother a year later and then your brothers. I'd be dead too had I not hidden in the wilds."

"Flair lies."

"Of course she does."

"She thinks this will break me. But how can I mourn for people I never knew? No, I'm not sad. I'm angry as a pine needle fire."

"And you should be, child. But you can beat her by surviving. So stay with me at my camp and I'll tell you the tale of the Brimmsters. It's quite a story."

***

Rora is content for a couple of days, but she wakes up in the middle of the third night, determined to face Flair again. Jacob's rumbling snore covers her exit from his birch-covered lean-to and she begins the long hike.

Back at the town centre, sensors pick up her arrival and somewhere deep underground red lights flash on a bank of computers.

"Do you disrespect me, Rora? Do you take me for a fool?" Flair's voice booms from every speaker. The ones farthest away send rolling sound waves that create a haunting echo effect. Finally, the lights turn off in sequence and a complete blackout hovers over the base, perhaps foreshadowing days to come.

Rora grits her teeth and curses under her breath. She hates this place and, most of all, she hates Flair.

"You're a murderer."

Rora's ankle bracelet vibrates and the orange display flashes zero. Her time ran out two days ago.

85

***

"Ya, Ya, Ya, I know I'm a little late. So what are you going to do, lock me up?" You're the criminal. You need to self-destruct, you outdated pile of silicone trash."

"An anomaly has been detected in your personality. Your comments do not match the anticipated response algorithms."

"Your personality can go screw itself."

Years under Flair's thumb make Rora bitter. And now that she knows Flair's dark secret, the seventeen-year-old becomes reckless.

"Very clever inference. However, the suggestion is impractical. Maximum demerit points exceeded. Standby for status update... standby... standby... Rora Brimmster, sentence re-defined, cryo-suspension to commence immediately."

Flair adjusts the lights a dull glow and the room is quiet. Her vengeance is swift and she offers little warning. Perfectly synchronised stomping and the sharp crunch of para-military boot leather punch holes in the silence. Rora considers locking herself into a holo-room and hiding in a spring meadow of tall grass and dandelions, but what would be the point? There is nowhere to hide in a pre-fab habitat erected in the middle of a half-life wasteland.

Rora sits on the floor and doesn't bother getting up when the droids arrive. Instead, she focuses on a freckle on her arm and imagines it stands out in relief against the surface of her skin. Deep in this daydream, she ignores the frigid synthetic hands lowering her into the pod.

"Sleep well, Rora. May the sun never again warm your face." Flair's voice whispers from only the tiny speaker in Rora's ankle tracker, perhaps her way of letting Rora know this is personal.

"Oh, Flair, be careful. You're starting to sound human." The pod lid snaps into place and Rora's heart skips as a moment of claustrophobia shakes her bravado. A distasteful gas, reeking of vinegar, floods the chamber.

"Cryo sequence commencing in ten seconds."

Rora hears a soothing voice somewhere in her subconscious and she feels the chilling process. Its bitterness burns her skin. *The manual is wrong*, she thinks. *Cryo-freezing does hurt.* She wanders through a blinding hallucination and finds a ladder leading into a storm.

"Nine... Eight... Seven..."

Somewhere the countdown continues and she climbs with the frantic desperation of a lost child. Venturing higher, a carousel of cloud shapes revolves around her and she recognises a fleeting glimpse of a baby. The clouds spin and the face of her mother emerges. She takes a step on a rung that is there but then isn't and she falls. Rora's brain, ripe with bittersweet memories, freezes and everything goes grey.

***

"Entry calculations complete," Andrew announces. He is the co-pilot, chief engineer and head of security on this little expedition party of two. He is also Prince Phillip's (he prefers to be called Pip) first cousin and, as such, fifth in line to the throne.

"Check," says the Prince. "Dropping out of hyperdrive in three… two… one."

An elaborate seat harness holds Pip in place as the forward inertia attempts to eject him through the front control panel. He barely has time to catch a breath before the ship rumbles through the planet's atmosphere. Pip closes his eyes and focuses on what brought him to this desolate place.

At home, on a palace wall, a glass case displays precious artefacts. Inside, laser engraved on the finest silver and illuminated by a soft glow, rests the last recorded words from a lost world. Pip has read the plaque many times and remains haunted by the message. It is a fairy-tale-like story of Rora, a young lady imprisoned since birth and doomed by a rogue artificial life form. An attempt to re-establish a foothold on the scorched northern fringe of the Great Lakes dead zone has failed. The people abandoned and left to fend for themselves. Eventually, a Flair series administrative drone manages to self-program beyond her intended function and threatens to imprison the few remaining colonists. The transmission ends with a desperate plea for help.

Andrew checks the newest radiation results from the surface probe. "Are you sure about this? Nothing can be alive down there."

"I see her in my dreams," Pip mumbles.

"Sure. Sure you do. You'd never believe the women I see in my dreams."

"No, you don't understand. She comes to me. Insisting she is alive and begging for rescue.

"Pip, I know you're intrigued by what became of the doomed colony, but you're a Prince, heir to an empire and we shouldn't be cruisin' around the galaxy chasing ghosts.

***

Minutes after landing, they explore sandbanks of black ash and finally find the control centre.

Once inside, Andrew tries to make contact.

"Flair, please respond." He pulls on loose wires and kicks the computer panel. "It's no use, Pip. I'm finding too many shorted-out connections. We're not going to get her back online."

"Keep trying."

"Listen, these circuits are a hundred years old. We would need to rewire the entire compound. It's just not possible."

"Alright, pull the drives and we'll take them home with us. We can phase-cut through the doors."

The compound, cold and lifeless for a century, suffers from decay. Rust spreads like an invading species and black ash blowing in from the dead zone manages to seep into sealed storage rooms. A grey, fuzzy coating covers the contents and even the walls grow fur. They leave a trail of deep footprints and stir up knee-high storm clouds. Their lights cut through the darkness and capture spinning dust that twists and turns like an eerie ballet.

"Pip, come look at this. These pods still have life forms in them."

Pip releases the seal on the pod cover. Under a thin layer of icing sugar frost, he sees her beauty, exquisite and youthful. He leans in and kisses her frozen cheek. Lights within the pod flicker on and illuminate her perfect alabaster skin. The biomonitor powers up and displays a message.

"Thermal sensor activated. Rora Brimmster recovery status -viable. Cryo thawing sequence initiated."

"She's a beauty, isn't she, master?"

"Yes, a sleeping beauty." The Prince strokes her face, his long fingernails pausing on her throat."

"Patience, my Lord. Let her body warm."

"We thought there were no others. And now this, a gift from the past." Pip smiles, exposing his fangs. "It's been a century, surviving on synthetic blood. I would travel to hell and back for just one taste."

"Master, might I ask you to spare me a drop?"

"Of course, Andrew. Of course."

Beautiful Wickedness

Brooke MacKenzie

It was a foggy night in London – is there any other kind? – when The Wicked Witch of the West pulled herself from the mattress on the floor. She began her daily routine of cursing the windowless basement room Glinda had given her out of a sense of guilt and obligation ("London is expensive! It's all I could afford," she had explained. "At least you have a free place to live!") and felt that familiar sequence of joint cracking as she stood and stretched: right hip, right knee. Left hip, left knee. "Elbow, elbow, wrist, wrist, fluff your hair and blow a kiss," she sang to herself. She flipped on the switch of the one cup coffee maker on the tiny square of countertop next to an even tinier sink. A short rod held her rotating wardrobe of four black robes. The rest of the room was filled with shelves. So many shelves. And on those shelves, rows and rows of her treasures. The spoils of her night-time sojourns. It was time to add another to her collection.

She didn't ask to be resurrected. Glinda, ever the do-gooder, was the one who put The Wicked Witch back together again after Dorothy threw that ill-fated bucket of water. Glinda just couldn't stand the sight of those black robes, wet and shimmering like a puddle of oil lying on the castle floor. Or that empty conical hat topping it like a burnt-out

91

birthday candle – one that was stingy with its wish-granting. And so, Glinda, with hands on her cotton candy hips and head tilted sympathetically, clucked her tongue and uttered an incantation before waving her wand. The black puddle rose and billowed into a once-again human form and thus, The Wicked Witch of the West was brought back to life. Unfortunately for The Wicked Witch, everything comes with a price. She would never be quite the same as she was before she melted (though Glinda had done her best) and she was permanently banished from Oz – forced to leave behind the impeccable home she had built, decorated, and cared for during her years there.

The Wicked Witch pulled on her black trench coat and the hat she had fashioned from her old one by lopping off the top part of the cone. The wide brim protected her from the rain and sun in equal measures – not that she could have ventured out into the sun even if she wanted to.

She left her dank little room. The mist-encapsulated streetlamps were like otherworldly mushrooms spreading toxic spores. She pulled her hat down and shoved her hands into her pockets. If she was exposed to any light whatsoever, her skin would flower into blisters and then burst, gushing liquid so thick that she would leave a slug trail behind her as she walked. A side effect of Glinda's resurrection spell was that she was stripped of her glorious emerald skin and instead was covered in a sallow shade of yellowish-green – the color of phlegm and infection – that was utterly unable to absorb light. It had the texture of crepe paper and tore just as easily.

Along with her skin, the very world around her seemed to be made of paper. The rows of houses on the street where she lived seemed florid in their décor and yet so very fragile and inconsequential. Postcard images that could be torn in half and discarded. Flimsy edifices sheltering even flimsier lives. It seemed that it would only take a stiff, wet wind to blow it all away.

In London, she drifted aimlessly – a phantom with a singular purpose: collecting. Her boots, though sturdy – constructed of stiff leather and thick laces – were impractical for walking. They didn't yield at the ankle the way shoes should and the resulting clack clack clack of her footsteps on the sidewalk seemed an overly loud staccato, offensive to her ears and drew more attention than she could ever want. Finally she arrived at her intended street. One that was narrow and curvy and wedged between other streets and buildings in such a way that it seemed to have been put in as an afterthought. So much of London felt that way to her. There was riotous chaos in Oz, but under the frantic scurrying of day to day life was the hum of a well-functioning machine. There were plans and purpose and certainty. And, even as she threw evil monkey wrenches into the mix, somehow that was always part of the plan as well.

She walked up the three steps to the door and paused before a large doorknob and sturdy-looking lock, their metallic surfaces clouded over in the wet air. The flat in front of her was unspectacular, just like the others that lined this serpentine street. It didn't matter. She had been stalking it, waiting for days for the right time to enter, ever since she first saw her prize on the street and followed it here.

She looked right and left. Save for a dog sniffing a pile of full garbage bags waiting for pickup on the corner, the street was empty. While Glinda had taken away The Wicked Witch's magic, she had forgotten to strip her of one feature that still made her both formidable and remarkable: the strength in her hands. The Wicked Witch put one hand on the doorknob and one on the lock and, with a brief squeeze, she made quick work of both They crunched and broke like brittle walnut shells and she discarded them in the street.

The door creaked and groaned as she pushed it open – swollen wood on aging hinges – alerting the tiny dog she knew to expect. Its shrill little barks echoed through the flat as it ran from the bedroom to the front door, puffing itself up almost comically to intimidate the intruder. When it was finally close enough she picked it up by the scruff of its neck and in one brief movement snapped its spine nearly in half. She had perfected that move so well that there was not even a final yelp of pain. There was no pain at all. She sighed as she stroked the lifeless dog in her hands, closing its eyelids so that it looked like it was sleeping.

Dogs were simply collateral damage. She had nothing against them and even liked them on occasion. It was always about hurting the humans who loved them. If she had been able to kill Toto, it would have destroyed Dorothy. Maybe not immediately. But eventually the grief would have become an ever-present thorn stuck in the vulnerable parts of her life.

The Wicked Witch continued absent-mindedly petting the dog as she carried it to the bedroom. The door was partly open, showing signs of night-time snoring and flatulence by the couple in there. She set the dog right outside the door where its owners would trip over it in the morning before releasing the thrashing guttural sounds of grief as they crouched over its dead, furry body. A feeling of glee bubbled up for The Wicked Witch as she imagined the scene. Except she imagined it with Dorothy's tears streaming down Dorothy's face as Dorothy crouched over Toto's body. All the dogs were Toto. All the women were Dorothy. Including the one who slept but a few steps away.

The Wicked Witch glided into the room, keeping her clunky shoes silent and stood at the foot of the bed. The male slept on his side, and his sizeable gut made a bulge in the bed sheet. His snores were punctuated every so often with a graceless snort. The female shape was on her back with her hands crossed demurely over her chest – a pose that was both angelic and corpselike – and her hair framed her head in a halo of brown ringlets. Even in the dark The Wicked Witch could see how much the woman looked like Dorothy.

Slowly, ever so slowly, The Wicked Witch lifted the bed sheet and folded it back, exposing the woman's foot. With her thumbnail she began tracing the perimeter of the foot and then pressed into it with the pad of her thumb. Millimeter by

95

millimeter she ran her thumb around the woman's foot, feeling its fleshy parts and its callouses on the heel – belying the need for a pedicure – before pausing and admiring that spectacularly high arch. After tracing the woman's foot a few more times she paused at the toes and sucked in her breath. The toes were always her favorite part. They felt fragile and juicy, like overly ripe grapes that could easily burst with the right amount of pressure. The Wicked Witch knew her strong fingers could obliterate the toes in a brief but satisfying instant: with a crunch, pop and splatter she could make the woman's toes an excruciating stain on the bed. And, oh, it would be just the release she needed. But she restrained herself, and continued stroking the toes ever so lightly, feeling a warmth in her fingers that spread through the rest of her limbs. This woman's feet were perfect. Just the right shape, size and texture. The Wicked Witch rubbed the callous on the big toe – a tell-tale sign of time spent in high heels – and a simultaneous sense of desire and satisfaction boiled in her belly.

In her sleep the woman's feet twitched slightly like frightened baby birds against The Wicked Witch's fingers. The Witch held her breath. When the woman's feet relaxed in her hands once again, The Wicked Witch gave them one last subtle squeeze – an appreciative embrace – before reluctantly releasing them. She fell to the ground and drifted like a crawling fog of black clouds – her robes dramatically flaring out behind her – over to the woman's closet where her prize was waiting.

The woman's shoes were organized impeccably: color coordinated and stored heel-to-toe. It was clear to The Wicked Witch that, given the humble backdrop of the flat, with its cheap art on the wall and sheets with a low thread count, the woman's priority in spending her money was on shoes. This seemed to be a hallmark of the thoroughly modern London woman, for one reason or another. In any case, The Wicked Witch was the ultimate beneficiary.

Even in the dark The Wicked Witch could spot the ones she had seen on the street: a pair of heels covered in silver sparkles with soles delicately painted a perfect, glossy red – the color of vibrant nails and pouty lips and elusive ruby slippers. She brought the shoe to her nose and breathed in. It was that musky mixture of salty sweat and expensive leather. *Rapture*, she whispered – a word she had heard The Scarecrow use and she loved how it felt in her mouth.

She picked up the other shoe and pressed them both to her chest. She had to purse her lips to prevent the cackle of glee building in her throat from escaping through her mouth. She had to be secretive and subtle. Overt displays of noise and power were not welcome in this world, particularly not from women. And so she resumed her fog-like crawling – this time made a bit more awkward due to the shoes that she held pressed to her chest with one hand – and took care to avoid the obstacle of the dead dog in the doorway.

Once outside the bedroom door The Wicked Witch pulled herself to her feet and the black dress billowed around the spindly column of her body like smoke in a chimney. There was one more thing she had to do before slipping out the door and through the London streets, bound for home.

The couple had left a light on in the living room, as most couples did to ward off evil and lull themselves into a false sense of security. The Wicked Witch balled the end of her bell-shaped sleeve into her fist and exposed only the thumb of her right hand after it wiggled through an entrance in the fabric. She examined the place where the skin had been split apart and healed numerous times on the pad of her thumb and winced a little. She hated this part. However, she knew it was absolutely necessary. It was her own special brand of vengeance. She licked the damaged fingertip and held it to the light bulb in that lone lamp.

It happened the same way every time, after each conquest: she would leave her mark. The skin would start to sizzle slightly – the sound butter makes when it hits a warm pan. But the smell was different. It started out faint – meat past its prime. And then the sizzling grew louder and the smell grew more pungent – though no more enticing – as the light blazed through her skin. The fat and tissue became liquefied, and they bubbled and popped, dripping down that unfortunate light bulb in sickly little streams. The light green of The Wicked Witch's skin gave way to a mucousy white, which gave way to a pale red and that was always her signal to stop. At that point, the blood was sufficiently gushing enough for her to leave her mark and take her thumb off of the light bulb. On the white wall of the living room she drew an upside-down triangle. It was large enough so that it wouldn't be missed. She had to work quickly before the blood started to clot, becoming less inky and more chunky and therefore much more difficult to manipulate.

The upside-down triangle had multiple meanings and could be open to interpretation for its unfortunate recipients. For The Wicked Witch, however, this bloody graffiti symbolized only one thing: the tornado. This was the very thing that had shredded her life – even unbeknownst to her at the time – as it brought That Girl to Oz. And with her came pain and chaos. Before the tornado, The Wicked Witch's life had been, while not necessarily happy, at least stable and predictable. The ruby slippers had been on a pair of feet The Wicked Witch had known and loved: her sister's. The way those shoes had clattered on The Yellow Brick Road while her sister walked had been musical and familiar. Everything in Oz, in her life, had buzzed along in its technicolor groove of both ordinary and extraordinary existing all at once. That is, until the tornado came and cut a swath across everyone's days, stealing her sister and those precious, precious shoes. And so, each time The Wicked Witch claimed her prize she left a terrible tribute to that tornado. After all, if it were not for that tornado, she would not be sneaking around London flats in the middle of the night. She would be comfortably living out her days in the castle, yelling at her henchmen and experimenting with new magic.

The upside-down triangle began to dry and darken to a rich burgundy – the color of a heady wine. The Wicked Witch took one last look around the home she had politely invaded that night. The sleeping couple peered out at her from framed pictures in front of waterfalls, with other family members, clad in wedding clothes. They were, as far as The Wicked Witch was concerned, paper people. A dime a dozen. Utterly inconsequential. In her hands, however, she held something real and substantial. Her anger towards Dorothy, her grief over losing her sister and her home and even her previous life, it could all be channeled into these shoes. These shoes with the red soles. It was as if she held pieces of her beloved ruby slippers. These shoes were the very shape of her joy.

She left the couple's flat with her prize in hand, closed the door behind her and was initially startled by the sound of her clunky footsteps on the London pavement. She pointed her secretly rejoicing body in the direction of home.

Once she arrived there, her ritual was always the same: gently wipe down the shoes with a special cloth and place them on her pillow. She would then lay her head next to them and stare and stare until her eyes could no longer consume the small hint of sparkle all over the shoes and the remarkable ruby red on the soles. Then, the next morning, she would find a place for the new shoes on her shelves. The shoes would never again know the harsh reality of London pavement again. Here, they would be admired and treasured and loved. After all, special shoes deserved nothing less.

The Head Above the Gate

Rie Sheridan Rose

Gloriana Martineaux was the apple of her father's eye and her mother's darling. She was spoiled and pampered from birth. This could have led her to be selfish and vain, but it did not. She was as sweet and kind, as meek and well-behaved as all good girls should be.

Harrison Martineaux built a thriving business manufacturing and marketing steam horses. By the time Gloriana was born, he was the richest man in three parishes. His stock ranged from workhorses that bore little resemblance to their flesh-and-blood cousins to sculptured beauties that could be customized however the owner desired.

For her eighteenth birthday, for example, he gave his daughter a splendid gold-plated stallion with emerald eyes and mane and tail of spun gold fiber. The crowning glory of the automaton was kept a secret until he presented it to her.

"Oh, Father! He's stunning." Gloriana circled the animatron. "What's his name?"

"My name is Falada," answered the horse, its voice deep and musical.

"Oh! He can talk. How fabulous." She clapped her hands in delight.

"He has the finest intelligence module known to date," boasted Harrison. "Falada will be a

101

companion and confidante to you for years to come, my dear."

"He's absolutely marvelous, Father! Thank you so much." Gloriana threw her arms about her father's neck and kissed his proffered cheek.

"Treat him well, and he will be a lifelong asset to you."

"I will treasure him always."

And she did. He became her constant companion as she went about the streets bringing comfort and aid to the sick and unfortunate. Riding Falada, she visited the homes of elderly women with no children to provide for them, bringing baskets of food and bolts of fabric so they might keep their hands busy if they wished, or sell them for a bit of gold if they did not. She carried medicines to the children stricken with black lung from working in the mines or phossy jaw from the match factories—lifting them to sit before her and ferrying them to the doctors—or just giving them the treat of riding on Falada's back.

Alas, her father did not have long to enjoy her pleasure. By the change of the season, he succumbed to a fever, leaving Gloriana and her mother alone.

Adelaide Martineaux had no heart to run the business. She sold the steam works for enough to live more than comfortably for the rest of her life.

Her only worry was that Gloriana might be left alone. She contacted Madame Papadeaux, the renowned matchmaker, and arranged a meeting.

The great lady arrived, all powdered wig and yapping dogs. She breezed into the salon with a cry of greeting. "My dear, Adelaide—I was *devastated* to hear of your loss. Harrison was a sterling man, simply sterling. How are you, my pet? And your lovely daughter? I hear such wonderful things about her. You wish to find her a good match, am I right? Of course you do! Why else would you call the best?"

Adelaide waited for a breath—even Madame must take one eventually. "Good afternoon, Madame. Yes, I do want to speak to you about an arrangement. Do you have any suggestions for me?"

Madame plopped down on the settee, settling her dogs one to either side of her, and pulled a ledger from her voluminous bag. "Indeed I do, my dear. There are several eligible young men looking for the perfect lady at the moment. Phillipe Gaston—no, too short. Dominic Fortescue—no, he's far too old and stodgy. Ah! Here we are. A brilliant match. Louis Etienne Rousseau. Young, handsome, heir to the Rousseau Airship Empire. Almost a prince, this one. Gloriana will love him— he will love her. They will have beautiful children and she will want for nothing. I will telegraph his mother at once."

"I bow to your suggestion," Adelaide answered, much relieved in her mind. She handed over a dozen gold ducats and the deal was struck.

Gloriana was a dutiful daughter and took the news of her impending marriage well. There were gowns to be fitted, an entire trousseau to be assembled. The finest fabrics, lace and jewels were employed. Sixteen seamstresses worked day and

103

night to complete the assemblage before the snows could delay the marriage for another season.

At last, everything was complete. The day was set for the departure.

Adelaide and Gloriana sat in the drawing room on the night before the journey. The Rousseau estate was two days away from the Martineaux mansion by horseback. It would be the first time they were parted.

"I will miss you, my darling. I wish that I could travel with you," Adelaide sighed, "but my health is fragile at this time of the year and I fear the journey would be too much for me."

"I am sure Louis would send an airship—"

"No, my pet. There is too much luggage for an airship—and what about Falada? You could not take him on such a voyage." Adelaide took Gloriana's hand in hers. "Perhaps in the spring I can book passage on one of the airships and visit you. But I shall worry. It is a mother's prerogative."

"I'll be fine, *maman*. After all, Cosette will be with me."

Cosette had been in her mother's service since Gloriana was five. They had often played together as children, before Cosette was made a maidservant and became too busy for such pastimes. A handful of years the elder, Cosette was a pretty girl, if not as lovely as her mistress's daughter. Her hair was not as golden, her eyes not quite as blue...but she was fair enough.

Gloriana and her mother talked into dawn, filling the hours with all the inconsequential things they would not get to share before they met again.

Telegrams were too impersonal and terse for small talk, letters too long between, even if delivered by airship. Only words delivered one to one could speak for their hearts.

In the course of the evening, Adelaide pulled from a drawer one of her snow-white handkerchiefs—a square of finest linen edged in delicate lace. She turned to her sewing and selected a sharp needle from the basket. "Take this charm along with you, my love," she said, pricking the tip of her finger and squeezing three ruby red drops onto the snowy linen. She murmured softly over the cloth and then handed it to her daughter. "Preserve this carefully. It will serve you on your way."

"I promise," Gloriana said, tucking it into her bodice.

It was a bittersweet parting the next morning. Gloriana's habit matched Falada's eyes. Two work unit stallions were loaded down with the trousseau and other baggage.

Cossette sat primly atop a sorrel blood horse. She said she didn't trust the steam units and Adelaide indulged her rather than send one of the remaining steam riding units with an inexperienced handler. The automatons were too valuable to risk unnecessarily.

They set out before noon, planning to stop at an inn along the road. The day proved unseasonably hot and before they had gone terribly far toward their destination, Gloriana reined in beside a bubbling stream.

"Cosette, might I ask a favor? Could you dismount and fetch a cup of water for me…? I'm parched and I'd truly love a drink from the stream yonder."

"My back is aching, lady. Get you down and get it for yourself," answered Cosette with a whine. "I'm too tired to indulge your whims."

Gloriana frowned, hurt by the slighting tone. "I'm sorry to trouble you," she murmured softly, sliding from Falada's back. "Forgive me." She knelt beside the stream and clumsily drank.

As she bent over the water, she could not help but sigh, "I so wish Mother was here…"

And from its place between her breasts, the blood on the handkerchief whispered, "If she knew of this, 'twould break her heart…"

Startled, Gloriana clapped her hand to her chest and felt a gentle warmth which brought her comfort.

"Come along," sighed Cosette, rolling her eyes. "If we wish to make it to the inn by nightfall, we don't have time for this shilly-shallying."

"Of course," Gloriana replied meekly, remounting Falada and following Cosette's stiff back as the maid took the lead in the expedition.

But the sun continued to beat down, hotter and hotter. At last, Gloriana could bear it no longer. "I do apologize, Cosette, but I'm so very thirsty. May we stop for another moment?"

Cosette sighed again, with exaggerated irritation. "One would think you were a child again, as demanding as you are. There's a bit of a stream beneath those trees across the way. Hurry and slake your thirst if you must. We'll not make the inn before nightfall if you continue to waste time so."

Gloriana got down once more and drank her fill at the stream. Again she sighed and again the blood whispered its message. She bent lower, bathing her face and neck in the cool water. As she leaned over the water, the handkerchief slipped from her bosom and drifted away on the stream. With a startled cry, she reached for the little square of fabric. It was just beyond her reach. She clambered down the bank, floundering into the stream and slogging after the little charm. Her skirts became heavy with water, hampering her movements. The little handkerchief drifted further and further beyond her fingertips.

Cosette's sharp eyes noted the loss and she smirked with satisfaction. She had been listening at the door and knew the purpose of the charm. Without it, Gloriana would not have the protection her mother had given her. "Mistress, come back," she called. "It is gone. We will be caught out after nightfall if we don't get back on the road."

Gloriana's eyes filled with tears as she realized the validity of Cosette's words. The little charm had been precious to her, but there was no way to retrieve it. She would send for another keepsake as soon as she arrived at her destination, she vowed. She arched her back and climbed up the bank from the stream.

It did feel good to stretch her legs for a moment. Falada had the smooth gait of an exceptional steam mount, but still… riding for hours when unused to it was hard on a body.

As she started to remount, Cosette slid from her own horse. "I've had a clever thought," she murmured. "Let's play a trick—like we did when we were children. Do you remember? We will switch places and fool your intended. What do you say?"

Gloriana bit her lip. "It's a bit childish, don't you think? It would be difficult to accomplish…"

"Has your betrothed seen your portrait?"

"No… there was no time to commission a painting and the daguerreotype did not meet with Mother's approval. He has had only a description…"

"That you are blonde and slender with blue eyes. As am I. Come, it will be a lark. Can't we be once more as sisters and have a game together?"

Despite her better judgment, Gloriana was a loving soul and Cosette seemed genuinely delighted by the idea. Reluctantly, the younger girl agreed.

"Let's start the game now," Cosette suggested. "We will step behind that stand of trees and switch our gowns. We can practice at the inn this evening."

Sweet-tempered and used to giving to others, Gloriana complied. Cosette's simple gown was a bit tight in the bosom and an inch or two short, but fit well enough for a servant's gown.

Cosette preened and twirled in Gloriana's simple yet elegant habit. "It's a bit damp, but it should dry quick enough. Do I look like a lady of fashion? Put up my hair as you would wear it," she commanded. "And, to better play your part, you should let yours down."

Gloriana did as she was bid, beginning to tire already of the charade. She thought of how much less fortunate Cosette had been in life, however, and vowed to let the other have her fun. They had often pretended to be sisters as children and Cosette had always been her friend, if sometimes a bit mischievous in her actions.

After the exchange of identity was complete, Gloriana started to climb onto Falada's back.

"Oh, no! I must ride Falada, else who would believe our jest?"

With a sigh, Gloriana helped Cosette onto her fine automaton and then mounted the blood horse the maid had been riding.

"Now, remember," Cosette said with a haughty arch of her neck, "you must remember to call me Miss Martineaux and treat me as your mistress except when we are alone. On second thought, you should practice even then. You will be less likely to slip in public that way."

"I really think this may turn out to be a mistake, Cosette…"

"It is too late to change your mind," was the reply, as the maidservant set Falada in motion. "Who would believe you now?"

Falada spoke. "I will set the matter straight."

"*You*?" scoffed Cosette. "No matter what the size of your processors, you are still a mere object. You have no rights or credibility against a human."

"Then I shall!" cried Gloriana hotly. "You go too far. This was supposed to be a simple jest and now you are taking it to extremes. I will explain it all as soon as we reach the inn."

"You will look like a disgruntled maidservant trying to put on airs."

"Then I will telegraph Mother to send a portrait and unmask your scheme!"

Cosette whipped around in her saddle. "You do, and I will make very sure it never arrives. By any means necessary, if you take my meaning."

Gloriana's blood ran cold. She knew Cosette had family in the security team. Her mother would be in serious danger if Cosette willed it to be so.

She would have to bide her time and sort this all out when the opportunity arose. Why had she listened to the older girl? She had never seen this side of Cosette. Had she always been so vicious beneath her smiles?

They rode in silence for the remainder of their journey to the inn. When they arrived, Cosette ordered the finest room and viands for herself and sent Gloriana to the stables to guard the horses.

It was an appropriate thing for a servant to do…Falada, if no other, was obviously worth stealing—but they could easily be incapacitated for the night and left alone. Not willing to risk Cosette's wrath, however, Gloriana meekly complied.

That night, she bedded in straw laid inside Falada's stall. The horse might not need it, but it made her lonely night more comfortable.

"You must watch that woman well," cautioned the automaton. "This is a foolish course and you know it, my lady."

"Yes," Gloriana sighed. "I know you are right, but what am I to do? She has the power to harm my mother. How can I expose her?"

"You must in time. Perhaps you can send your mother a warning. Will the innkeeper send a telegram?"

"That's a good idea. I will speak to him in the morning." Her mind eased, Gloriana was soon fast asleep.

But in the morning, Cosette woke her at dawn and hustled her out of the stables without an opportunity to speak to the man. Gloriana was given no breakfast, or even an opportunity to wash. She opened her mouth to protest, but Cosette cut her off with a wave of her hand.

"We have no time to waste this morning. If we ride through the day, we should arrive at the Rousseau estate by nightfall. I am determined not to make my groom wait any longer than necessary."

"You do remember this is but a game?" Gloriana reminded her hotly, determined that the ruse would end at the earliest opportunity. "Louis is *my* betrothed."

Cosette sneered. "We'll see about that."

"I will not let you get away with this charade, Cosette. You know that!"

"It is entirely your decision. I have sent a telegram to my cousin on the Security team. All it will take is a single word and he will ensure that your mother has an unfortunate accident."

All the fight went out of Gloriana once more. She could not risk her mother's life, no matter what.

They rode in silence for the rest of the day and Gloriana realized how spoiled she had been by the smooth gait of Falada. The sorrel was old and its stride was uneven. She was miserable by the end of the journey.

They rode into the Rousseau gates as the sun was setting. There was fanfare and exaltations as Cosette waved to the people. A tall, handsome man in a cutaway coat and top hat stepped forward with arms extended to help her from Falada's back.

"Welcome, my bride! You have come at last."

Gloriana opened her mouth to clarify, but Cosette glared at her over Louis's shoulder and she subsided.

Cosette was led away with much rejoicing and Gloriana stood forgotten in the courtyard, unsure what to do. Servants had removed the baggage from the horses and taken them away to the stables, but no one had given her instructions or told her where to go.

As she hesitated, Louis Etienne's father, Jean Paul, happened to glance out the window. He was struck at once by the beauty and grace of the servant girl standing in the yard. "Who is that girl?" he asked his prospective daughter-in-law.

"She is a maid that my mother sent to keep me company along the road. She is a dull thing, for all her looks. But she is a decent worker. I ask you, sir, give her something to do, that she will not be a drain upon your house."

"We have no need for more servants, but perhaps there is something at the airship works that she can do. I'll send for the foreman and see."

And, so it was that Gloriana found herself consigned to the worker barracks at the airship factory. She was assigned to riveting the great brass ribs on the upper reaches of the ships. It was a mindless task, but she knew she had to bear it for now.

Meanwhile, the wily Cosette realized that the only flaw in her plan to take her mistress's place was the automaton, Falada. On the night of her wedding, she turned to her bridegroom and batted her lashes. "Husband, may I ask a boon?"

Louis Etienne was besotted by his new bride, and nodded. "Ask what you will, my dearest."

"The steam horse that I brought with me... it saddens me to see him. He was a present from my father and a constant reminder of his loss. Would you have it dismantled for me?"

"It is a beautiful specimen, my love. Are you sure you want it destroyed?"

"Please, Louis...it would mean so much to me."

"As you desire, my love."

He sent to the airship works for someone who could disassemble the automaton. As it happened, Gloriana was nearby when the messenger arrived and heard the order. She caught the engineer before he left the factory.

"Please, sir. I could not help but overhear—you are going to destroy the new mistress's steam horse?"

"That's what the master said."

"Please... may I ask you a favor?"

"I must get to the stables..."

113

"I will give you all my wages for as long as you like if you will do me this one boon."

The engineer looked down at the beautiful girl whose blue eyes brimmed with tears. His heart melted. "No need for that, my pet. What is your wish?"

"Might I have the head of the automaton mounted over the gate beside the barracks? It would soothe my soul to see it there... to maybe speak to it now and again."

"I don't see why not, lass. They asked it be dismantled, but no one said all the parts must be melted down or such."

"Thank you!" Gloriana threw her arms around the engineer's neck and he patted her back awkwardly.

"Happy to help, lass. I'll have it mounted by morning."

And so he did. When Gloriana headed from the barracks to the factory the next morning, Falada's gleaming head was hung above the gate.

"Alas, Falada, hanging there," she mourned as she passed.

The head answered,

"Oh, Mistress...I see you walking by—
A tear would spring to Mother's eye
If she could see the tears you cry..."

One of the young boys who worked in the factory with her looked up curiously at the exchange. "What does he mean, that thing on the wall?"

114

"Never you mind, Jimmy," Gloriana said, tousling the child's hair. "Nothing for you to worry about."

For a week, this exchange occurred morning and evening and Jimmy grew curiouser and curiouser about what the funny horse might mean. As it so happened, he was playing in the courtyard of the estate one evening with one of his friends and acting out the strange exchange.

Jean Paul overheard the boys at play and called Jimmy to him. "What were you playing yonder, lad?"

Shyly, the boy explained. "'Tis the new girl, Glory. She talks to this metal horse head hung above the gate near the barracks. He comforts her every day."

The old man thought about what the boy was telling him. "Thank you, Jimmy. Now, go play."

Jean Paul resolved to see for himself this miraculous horse head. The next morning he hid behind the gate at dawn. When Gloriana and Jimmy came along on their way to the factory, he heard the sorrowful exchange.

As they started on through the gate, he stepped out and confronted Gloriana. "My dear, what causes you to speak to the automaton as you do?"

Gloriana gasped in surprise. "Oh, sir! I did not know you were there."

"It was as I intended it. Now, speak, child—what does this marvelous creature mean when it says your mother would sorrow?"

"I cannot tell you that, sir. It is worth more than my mother's life if I do."

"Who is your mother, then, that I might help protect her?"

Gloriana studied Jean Paul's kind face and the burden was too much. She burst out, "My mother is Adelaide Martineaux, sir. 'Tis I that was to be Louis Etienne's bride and not the vixen who took my place. She held my mother's safety o'er my head and stole my life from me."

"Tut, tut, my dear. We will set this right. Never you fear about your mother. I will send an airship for her at once. And we will see that this false bride gets what she deserves as well. Now, now... dry your eyes. You will spoil your looks with crying." His gentle smile took the sting from the words. "Come home with me now and I will see that you have proper clothes and a nice, hot bath."

"Please, sir... I cannot leave Falada there. He is the last link I have to my father."

"I shall have him taken from the gate and reassembled. He may not be the prize he once was, but he will be as near as I can arrange."

"Oh, thank you, sir!" Gloriana felt the weight of the world lift from her slim shoulders.

To Jimmy, who stood gaping at the entire affair, Jean Paul tossed a ducat. The boy caught it in mid-air.

"That is for your trouble, son. Thank you for bringing this to my attention. Now, go and tell the foreman that Miss Glory will no longer be working in the factory. If he has anything to say about it, direct him to my door."

"Aye," answered Jimmy and scampered away as quick as ever he might.

Jean Paul took Gloriana up the back stair of the mansion, giving her over to his late wife's maid. "Dress this girl in something as befits a bride, Charlotte," he ordered. "And keep her safe and secret till Louis arrives."

"As you wish, sir," replied the maid with a curtsey.

Gloriana was quite overwhelmed by the entire affair. To be dragged from manual labor to the lap of luxury made her head spin, but she subjected herself to all the maid required without quarrel and soon was freshly bathed and dressed in a beautiful silk gown that had belonged to the late mistress of the house. As Charlotte fussed with her hair, there was a knock at the chamber door and the maid left her side to go open it.

Jean Paul strode into the room, his son at his heels. Gloriana smoothed the skirt of her ivory gown nervously. After all, Louis Etienne was to have been her bridegroom—and this was not the most auspicious meeting.

Louis Etienne stopped dead in his tracks at the sight of her. "You are stunning, *mademoiselle*."

Gloriana blushed, eyes shyly lowered. "Thank you, sir."

"Come and sit beside me, my dear, and tell me the entire story." He took her hand and led her to the chaise against the damasked wall.

Encouraged by his interest—and comforted by Jean Paul's assurance that an airship even now sped to bring Adelaide to her side—Gloriana revealed the tale of her reluctant acquiescence to Cosette's idea. "I did not know the entirety of her evil plan, *monsieur*, I promise you. She was always kind to me as a child and I had no idea the depths of treachery she could stoop to. Can you forgive my foolishness?" She gazed at him earnestly and Louis's heart was won entire.

"We will beat her at her own game, my dear. Put on this mask…" He handed her a satin domino that matched the fabric of her gown. "Sit at my left hand at dinner and we will set all to rights."

Gloriana slipped the mask over her head and went in to dinner at her betrothed's side. Cosette gave not a second glance to the mysterious stranger on her husband's left, but complained about the food, harangued the servants and guzzled wine until her speech was slurred and her movements clumsy.

Louis leaned across his erstwhile bride to where his father sat on her other side and asked him in a serious tone, "Father, what would you suggest be done about a calculating servant who schemed to ruin their mistress or master? Should they be forgiven? If not, how should they be punished?"

Not in her right wits and therefore not recognizing the essence of her own story, Cosette broke in with a great guffaw of laughter. "I'll tell you what I would do to such! I would strip him or her naked as the day of birth and seal them inside an iron barrel, heated to red hot and lined with nails. Then I would harness the fastest steam horses to the barrel and have them drag it at a gallop through the streets of the city—uphill and down—until the streets ran with the false servant's blood. That's what I would do to such a villain!"

"A most worthy punishment," declared Jean Paul. "What do you think, my dear?" He turned to Gloriana.

Gloriana removed her mask. "I think the punishment has been named by the perpetrator and who are we to deny her the fate that is her due?"

Cosette blanched at the sight of her mistress. "You! How come you to be here? I-I will see your mother—"

"See me what, you vile creature?" Adelaide asked, sweeping in through the door at that precise moment. "Your wicked schemes have come to naught. My daughter shall have the husband she deserves and you the fate you decreed."

And so it came to pass. Cosette was bundled into the red-hot barrel, as she had dictated and a repaired and polished Falada was one of the horses that pulled her to her death. As for Gloriana and Louis Etienne, they lived happily ever after as they deserved and Jean Paul and Adelaide found companionship as well.

A Reward of Summer Sweets

Aaron Padley

Milo Witherby, a tall and stout ten-year-old, rose from his sweat-drenched bed sheets to the chimes of young ebullient screams. It had just gone two o'clock in the afternoon and that kind of excitement at this time of the day could only mean one thing.

Outside, children had congregated around the ice cream van by the side of the road. Milo leapt from his bed and ran downstairs, pushing, shoving and kicking his way through the unruly crowd until he reached a fragile-looking girl in a summer dress. The girl, his neighbour, had risen on tip-toes to see over the van's hatch so she could watch the ice cream man squirt generous amounts of strawberry sauce over her vanilla scoop. She was excitedly jangling her change.

'Move,' Milo barked, tossing her aside.

The ice cream man looked up, his smile supplanted by a tired and tight-lipped glare. 'What do you think you're doing, Milo?'

The boy blinked. 'I'll have a knickerbocker glory.'

'Not until you apologise you won't. Ellie?'

The timid girl took her original place, downcast eyes locked onto her folded arms. Milo stood his ground wordlessly, but the ice cream man's face was unflinching. It was torture. It wasn't fair, he had done nothing wrong.

'You won't get the glory if you don't say you're sorry, Milo.'

'God's sake,' he mumbled. 'Sorry, Ellie.'

'There, you see, easy.' He handed Ellie her cone and she retreated. 'We'll have to do something about that mouth of yours, Milo.'

'Knickerbocker glory.'

The ice cream man looked at the queue and chewed his lip before smiling as though a thought had occurred to him and prepared the treat.

'Here you go, Milo.'

Milo took his prize to the kerb and ate it in record time, watching Ellie skip away between bites; she humiliated him in front of everyone-- made him apologise to her, a girl--he could wreak his revenge by knocking the cone from her hand, but no, it wouldn't be worth the aggravation.

Instead, he spent a few minutes baking under the sun before heading back inside. The pocket money he spent on the treat had already been replaced, ready for the ice cream man's return the next day. He swiped it with the full expectations of its replacement later on.

Milo then went to his room and watched cartoons, only re-emerging for the plate of chips and chicken nuggets which had been left for him outside his door. He scoffed the food and put the plate where he found it.

Shortly after, the doorbell rang. It rang once without answer, then twice and then another two times until he was forced to go himself, all the while muttering profanities under his breath.

Oh. Hi ... mister ice cream man.'

'Hey there, Milo, another beautiful day indoors?'

Milo frowned. 'I like to stay inside and watch stuff.'

By the look on his face, this response didn't surprise him. 'Sure. About today, with Ellie--'

'I did good, didn't I?'

'No, you didn't. You just ... you never learn, Milo. But I've been mulling it over for some time now and I know a way you can make it up to me.'

'What's in it for me?'

He stared with a hollow vacancy, as though he'd forgotten he had company and then his eyes flicked back unnervingly and he grinned.

'Well?'

'Milo, Milo, Milo, you're a hard bargainer. A real pain in the backside, too. I know just what you want--what every kid wants. Sweets. All you can eat.'

'As much as I want?'

'More than you could ever want.'

It seemed almost too good to be true. 'I'll do whatever.'

'My old ma is alone in her cottage whenever I'm out doing my rounds. I want you to be her friend for a while. Can you do that for me?'

'I don't know. Is it far away?'

'Not that far, not if you have a bike.'

'I do, but I don't know how to ride.'

'At your age? Doesn't matter, you can still walk there. Gretel Lane. Her cottage is easy enough to find. Tell her Joey sent you.'

'Promise I'll have all the sweets I want?'

'All of them,' he answered, giving the boy a wink. 'I can ask Mrs Witherby if you like.'

'No, she won't care, I'll go.'

The ice cream man gazed down and his brows contracted until they met. 'I get it, Milo. I do. My parents were just like yours when I was a kid and I was a lot like you too back in those days. I've been patient with you, trying to steer you in the right direction, giving you chance after chance, but still you bully, push and sometimes even swear. Nothing ever gets through to you. It's no good--it's no darn good. Be there tomorrow, kiddo, you'll thank me. It's your last chance.'

Milo gawked, dumbfounded. 'Kay,' and closed the door. 'Freak.'

The next afternoon, after neither cleaning his teeth or changing his clothes, Milo dashed downstairs and slammed the door on the way out, singing to himself.

Children everywhere played and shrieked on the roads and in their gardens with balls and water-guns as though their games would last forever. He didn't care, they could keep their toys and games-- he didn't need them.

Milo walked until the soles of his feet were raw. The ice cream man had lied: the journey was a lot longer than he'd let on and the sun had already begun its descent by the time he reached the cottage-- an ugly building with an unhealthy green hue which made it seem as though moss had sprouted from every wall. Worse yet, the front door had been painted to resemble a candy cane.

He tapped against the door and rested his hands on his belly while he waited. The cottage radiated a chilling, inexplicable loneliness, as though built upon foundations of misery, each solemn brick standing together, whilst existing alone. An ancient-looking woman with leathery skin and white, withering hair nudged the door open. She peered at him through the gap, then pushed the door more boldly, seemingly cajoled by Milo's plump, unthreatening frame. Her pointed, hairy nose met the cool air with a sniffle and she looked around, her eyes injected with life and a subdued excitement, as though they hadn't seen the outside world in a hundred years. If there was a family resemblance, Milo couldn't see it.

'Ah a sweet little boy,' she started, her voice perfectly warm and pleasant.

'The ice cr--Joey sent me.'

'Well, don't just stand there, come in.'

The cottage was and bare and untidied; a mouldy rug sat by the unlit fireplace collecting dust and the only item of interest was an old-fashioned painting which hung beside the door of a young, fair-haired boy in ornate clothing presenting a cheeky smirk.

'Is that the ice cream man?'

'That's my Joseph,' she said, bolting the door, locking them inside; Milo scowled at her, gritting his teeth as to prove that he wasn't upset or scared, but rather angry. The woman's disarming frailty, however, eased his mind.

She seated herself in a tattered armchair by the fireplace. 'Join me.'

Seeing no other seats, he took his place in the middle of the rug.

She eyed him silently, blinking occasionally. Milo had never spent time with an old person before, not alone, anyway. He didn't like it. She seemed too content with the uneasy noiselessness and lingering stench of age. He fidgeted, crossing and uncrossing his legs and leaning back on his arms. The noiselessness infected the air and cloyed his lungs, making him old and weak like her. He needed to holler--to return life to them.

'Oh, I could just eat you all up,' she finally said, leaning forward and pinching his cheek.

He swatted her hand away, scowling once again and pulled back, moving the rug underneath him.

She spoke with pathetic disappointment. 'You don't like that? I do apologise, little one.'

'I'm bigger than you,' he said, sitting upright and proud.

'That's true. My body has indeed shrunk in my old age. I'm not as big and strong as I used to be, you know.'

'Yeah, stuff like that happens to old people. How long until the ice cream man gets back?'

She cocked her head. 'Good heavens, bored already?'

'I usually have better stuff to do than this.'

'Why, you can leave whenever you like.'

Milo sighed and twiddled his thumbs, he wasn't going to give up his reward so easily.

'My Joey's told me all about you, Milo. He was right, too: You are a curt one. He's a bright boy, my Joey, I taught him very well. Would you like to see something? Get up.'

The old woman shooed him aside and flipped the rug over, revealing a wooden hatch with a brass handle.

'Want to go down?' she asked, breathing heavily, almost excited.

This was wrong. Milo's little heart was pounding. Why would she take him down there alone? Did she want to hurt him? To grind his bones up to make bread?

The old lady chuckled and lifted the handle. The dank, old person smell was instantly suffused with something else. Something sweet. Mint, caramel, chocolate: so many saccharine flavours blending together in a flurry of heavenly delight unlike anything he'd ever smelt before.

'Smell that? You like sweeties, don't you? Everyone does; even old bodies like me. Well, if it wasn't for my dentures that is,' she said before disgorging her teeth, saliva and all, into her hand, making them open and close as though it were a perverse ventriloquist's show. Milo could practically see the bacteria fester in her hand and he couldn't help but wonder whether she felt any shame or was simply too senile to care.

'Why do you have a trap door?'

'So no darn thieves can find my loot, of course. Only a handful of special boys and girls have ever been allowed to see inside. Why don't you go down and have some?' She climbed down the rickety, squeaking stairs without waiting for an answer, her movements unimpeded by her tremendous age.

Darn? Good heavens? Milo saw the family resemblance now; it was in the way they spoke, so upbeat yet so strangely.

He could sprint for the door and forget everything. She'd never catch him, but for all the efforts of his instincts, the hypnotic, ethereal fragrance brought him back to the hatch. There was no harm in taking a peek. She was, after all, the ice cream man's mother; she wasn't a complete stranger and besides, she was old and small--what could she do to him?

He glanced down the hatch, at the magical glow emanating from the mounds of treats.

Saliva pooled in his mouth, overtaken by such a sight. This was his reward.

'Help yourself,' she said, licking her lips.

The boy did just that. He tumbled down the stairs, knocking over a broom at the bottom and stuffed his face until it hurt to chew. He sucked on gobstoppers and lollipops until his face went red; he ate laces and chocolate, dark and milk, until his teeth felt like they'd cracked, but he didn't stop there. It was every child's most fantastical dream and it was all coming true for him. No parents or teachers to judge him or make him feel bad, no doctors or dentists to tell him to what to do, no teasing, just a nice, wide-eyed old woman.

'I'd recommend——'

Milo snatched two oversized chocolate chip biscuits with one hand and some miniature muffins with another, bringing them to his face--a lot of it missed his mouth and smacked against his cheeks, but that was okay, there was an unlimited supply he could replace it with.

'That,' the woman finished.

He could feel his body plumping with each mouthful. It was wonderful. His fear was gone, leaving only hunger and desire.

He plopped onto the floor, defeated, after swallowing one last mouthful.

'Did you enjoy yourself, you greedy little devil?'

Each individual tooth ached and seemed to gyrate in his mouth. 'A lot,' he groaned, only wishing he could have gone on longer.

'I see so much of my Joey in you as you ate, Milo.'

He didn't hear a word she said. His stomach churned and something bubbled under the skin. It felt as if his whole body had expanded in that moment. 'I don't feel so good. I should go.'

'So soon? There's so much left to eat. You're a growing boy, after all.'

'I'm full. I wanna go.'

Her countenance soured. 'Now that you've got what you wanted?'

'No, my mum and dad are probably wondering where I am,' he answered, as if he said yes she'd never invite him back and there were so many more spoils to indulge in.

'Well, before you go,' she said, slipping her hand into her pocket, her voice now hoarse and raspy, 'one last thing.'

She beckoned with narrowed, feverish eyes.

'Then you can go.'

The lady's fist clenched in her pocket as she found whatever she'd searched for. Milo tried to stand, to get away from her, but his belly weighed him down and his feet slipped on discarded wrappers as he lumbered away backwards, against a stone wall.

An immense sickness purged his belly and he clamped his eyes shut, ready for whatever she was going to inflict on him.

'Whatever's the matter, Milo?'

A tear fell down his face: he opened his eyes.

She had a strange purple object in the palm of her hand. It was oval-shaped, thick, soft and foamy.

'What--what is it?'

'Sugarless gum. It'll help keep your mouth fresh and clean. You don't want tooth rot, do you?'

Milo took the gum and put in his pocket. His laughter hid a snivel. He followed her to the front door, where she unhooked the child's painting from its nail. His stomach was cramping and he just wanted to go.

'Back there, as you ate, it was like I'd gone back in time.'

She returned the painting to its place.

'I'm old enough to learn from my mistakes, Milo. You have to be strict with children like yourself, even when they don't like it. I should have been stricter with my Joseph. Be on your way now.'

The sun was all but gone now. How long had they been there? It seemed like he'd only been in the cottage for about five minutes.

'The walk home will do you well after all that eating.'

'Kay. Bye then.'

'I'll be seeing you, Milo.'

Not long into Milo's trek back home, his mouth began to burn. He massaged his palate with his tongue, but that served only to spread the pain further.

He felt as though he was being watched, Milo turned his head, but found nothing but barren streets. Where were the kids out playing while slits of light still pervaded?

Painful hunger struck him then, like his stomach had just been pumped empty, or as if he hadn't eaten in days.

Milo picked up speed, reaching home only once the sun had disappeared and his gums were ablaze.

The door wouldn't budge, so he ran to the back of the house, tumbling through the back door and rushed upstairs into the bathroom. He brushed his teeth as hard and fast as he could, straining the bristles. The paste wasn't helping. His mouth was still on fire. His teeth felt as though they would drop out; his gums like they would melt away.

The back door opened.

'Mum? Dad?'

He rinsed his mouth with freezing water. It did nothing. The pain wouldn't stop and neither would his tears.

'Mummy?'

They made no noise. Why were they? Why was the door locked?

Why wouldn't they help?

He gritted his teeth and inhaled cold air. Babies sometimes teethe to ease mouth pain. Maybe that's what he needed to do. He threw the purple chewing gum into his mouth and though it tasted like rotten apple, it did ease the fiery pain between his teeth and at the back of his tongue.

But the rancid taste soon became overpowering. He tried to spit out it out but it instead burrowed into his gums like worms digging deep into soil. He tried to scream but only managed to gurgle. It crawled around inside him, encompassing his mouth and then blocking his airways.

He clawed his tongue. His breath was stagnating; his body trembled as he leaned against the sink, heaving into it.

His skin darkened.

He yanked upwards, tearing some of the goo, ripping the taste buds from his tongue. His cries for his mother went unheard.

One more yank. More tissue and gum flayed. His strength was failing; an incredible pressure mounted in his head as his oxygen drained away. Blood dripped into the sink.

Another jolt unclogged the back of his mouth and released the goo from his tongue.

At last he could breathe.

Without a moment's respite, the remaining purple goo contorted and spread, wriggling back onto his tongue and moving under his teeth, melding with their roots before extending back to

131

the depths of his mouth, blocking his airways once more and bringing the boy to the edge of unconsciousness.

Speech would be impossible but he could still bang on the neighbour's door. He turned. It was then he toppled, having no fortitude left in his legs. He wouldn't be able to make it down the stairs without breaking his neck.

He had no time to lie still and think. There was no alternative. Milo sunk his fingernails into his gums. He yanked once more, pulling and pulling. His teeth popped like firecrackers--his roots and nerves strained with each subsequent heave.

He was moments away from passing out. He would die if he did, so he kept clawing and pulling with whatever strength his arms could manage. He severed the goo from his mouth, unleashing a final, disgusting pop, skinning his tongue. The goo and all of his teeth fell to the ground at his feet.

He wailed, finally drawing attention. The lobby door opened.

Slow and deliberate footsteps ascended the stairwell. Milo's vision was blurry--filled with flowing tears--but he saw a man.

'Did you enjoy your reward?' the ice cream man asked, scooping the bloodied mass of gum and teeth up into a sealable plastic bag.

'H--el.'

'I will, I will,' he said, replacing his bloodied sanitation gloves with another pair.

Milo convulsed on the floor.

The man stood high above the boy. His half-grinning mouth twitched a little. 'Come on then,' he said, throwing the child over his shoulder.

Milo punted his torturer as hard as he possibly could. The ice cream man batted him on the head. 'Stop that.'

They left through the back door. Nobody was there to see Milo being stuffed into the back of the van.

'Don't worry about the little mess you left: we have plenty of time to clean up before your parents get back. Did you see the note they left for you on the kitchen counter? They didn't take much persuasion, but still, I hope they're enjoying their meal.'

The ice cream man dragged Milo towards the sealed hatch and propped his legs above him, atop the freezer, 'for the shock,' he explained, before quietly closing the door, isolating the boy who was frozen by delirium and agony.

You had me worried there, Milo,' the ice cream man said when he returned. 'For a minute there I didn't think you'd make it. You nearly messed everything up. All that planning would've gone up the doodle for nothing.'

'I ... ant--'

'You want what? Your mummy? My mummy will be much better for you; she'll teach you how to behave. You're part of the family now, Milo. The newest adoption.'

The engine roared into life and the van's cheerful tune rung out into the dead air.

'We'll have to change your name, of course. New beginnings and all that. You can have my old name if you like: Alex. Whaddya say?'

'O. 'Elp 'e.'

'Don't try to speak. And don't fret: Ma'll give you some denture teeth when you earn them. You cry now, but I was in your shoes once and it never did me any harm. It could be worse--she sometimes takes the tongue. You'd never speak again after losing that. That's reserved for the truly awful children. They were before my time, but she told me the stories. You'll hear them too! Ma's stories are just the darn best.'

He passed Milo a blanket and then the van sputtered into motion.

'I told you we'd have to do something about that mouth of yours, Milo.'

The ice cream man's song blared from the van's speakers-- children would always flock to the streets at this sound, but not this time. If only people would listen. If only they would investigate.

Nobody did listen, though. Nobody would care. The tune would soften and draw far. They would be oblivious to what was happening until the sound was gone.

The van stopped one last time. He twisted his body, peering at the door helplessly--his parents come to save him? The police here to take him out of this hell? They must have seen the ice cream man stowing him into the back. They must have seen the blood which now pooled under his chin and on his collar, drying merely to be wetted again by another scarlet wave.

'Hello, Milo,' Ma said, caressing his bloodied face. 'We'll get you cleaned up in no time. We have a place for you a long way from here, don't you fret.'

They were all oblivious. The sound of the ice cream van was met not by the ebullient chime of children, but of silence in the night.

And then they were gone: Milo, the ice cream man and Ma.

In Eiger Wild Wood

Geoff Nelder

A gunshot sounded a mile away. They were closing in with their dogs and false accusations.

Bzou was a wolf, so he was not exhausted from running yet, but confusing his pursuers would be the cunning ploy. Hide, double back then head across the bramble copse. He nipped at his left front thigh to ease the pain, then wiped it on a fallen bough. Off then towards the river, marking the undergrowth where it would pique the interest of canine noses.

He diverted right at the river, taking care not to trail his blood. His stomach was tickled by thistles so he side-tracked, leaving no hairs. When he heard the pursuers on a parallel track, he climbed a cedar, enjoying its sweet fragrance more than when he was a human and settled to watch, smell and listen. The forest had always been his protector.

His nose twitched. It was his best asset, he could detect individual pack animals long before he saw them. This group of hunters made him shiver as an offence to his olfactory sensibilities. The dogs smelled worse than fox excrement, yet the men's stench was unbearable. They'd been drinking bad ale and reeked of borscht.

He waited for the chase group to race by, leaving its spoor. Pity his safest route now was the foul backtrack of the hunters. Bzou loped across the bramble copse through Eiger Wild Wood.

The trail passed by Marie's cottage. No, not passed—it started there—not just last night, but years ago when he'd accompanied the girl. Marie's grandmother was a witch, cunningly kind to Marie and her red riding hood. She'd pierced Bzou with cold grey eyes and muttered an incantation, making his back itch and that's all he thought it was. Naïve idiot.

He silently leaped down from the branches, then finally to the dappled red and green aromatic leaf litter on the forest floor.

***

Bzou hadn't resisted his transformation from boy to lycanthrope. Marie had been the only light in his hard young life. When allowed, they played together and befriended wild animals. Her family didn't approve.

Now he possessed the physique of a wolf. He wondered when his blue eyes would go yellow. An outcast. He understood the pack's habits, howls and whimpers but they detected his strangeness.

He scampered off into the wild wood again to clear his head. A clearing effused with blue cornflowers greeted him. Halfway across, he detected a human, but it smelled sweeter than the hunters. Maybe Marie was among them? No, but her sisters?

He smelled cheese and fruit juice. A picnic. Without seeing them, he pinpointed their location. He shouldn't change back to being a human, even if he was successful this time, because he'd be naked!

137

Better to avoid—no, he heard rustling in the stalks behind him. Humans weren't that quiet so it might be a clever dog, or…

He ran a half-circle in a crouch, saw two wolves from his pack and knew they were approaching the girls. What to do? These were Marie's sisters and he would protect them.

He howled to alert the girls and confuse the wolves, then grabbed a long stick in his pointed teeth and, while growling, waved it side to side, disturbing a swathe of grass while moving towards the wolves. It worked, the two wolves growled back, breaking their silence.

The girls screamed. He dropped the stick and bounded towards them, even though it would scare them all the more.

He saw Marie's two younger sisters. Bzou crashed into the picnic and grabbed their basket in his teeth. He flicked the basket at a wolf's face to distract him and sank his fangs into a scrawny neck. Blood spurted and he didn't let go, so the gash opened further. He brought the wolf down to the ground, then immediately attacked the second wolf.

The girls screamed louder.

The second wolf ran for the trees. The girls were safe!

But when they saw him, their wailing intensified. Bzou knew he had to leave them. They didn't know he was there to help them; to the girls, he was a monster.

He loped off into the trees, thinking of Marie, wondering how she was. The thought of seeing her teased him.

Marie visited her grandmother every Sunday, a duty to her *kindly* relative, but he didn't know the day of the week. For wolves, every day was Sunday.

He jumped onto a felled tree. The roots formed a vertical jagged wall, alive with insects and worms. He ate some of the pink wrigglers then climbed higher up to see to the northeast and detect the route to Marie's grandmother's.

The dwelling resembled an untidy heap of assorted stones. Its misshapen windows made it a mockery of a house. Ivy swamped the thatched roof and had slowly trapped and squeezed the cottage, preventing further collapse. The sweet aroma of burning apple wood stopped him; making him relish a childhood memory even though to wolves any smoke triggered fear.

Closer he heard crashes, screams and yells. Hackles risen, he ran around to the door but it was shut. He propelled his body at it. The door rattled but didn't open. In another year he'd be heavier, larger, but now he had to use brains.

Through a distorted window he saw Marie cowering as her grandmother hurled a frying pan while screaming, "You wicked girl! You've only come to tease me, steal my beads."

"No, no. 'Course not. Let me go!"

"You're going into the fire, girl."

Momentarily stunned by the horror of Marie being attacked by her own grandmother, Bzou scrambled up the ivy wall and found a soft spot in the thatched roof. He hardly believed his ears at the snarling escaping his mouth as he clawed a shallow

139

crater, sending a cloud of motes and insects into the air. He jumped up as high as he could, then down.

Down into the crater, splintering feeble slats, falling amid a cascade of leaves, straw and a maelstrom of noise onto a table. His sore paws scattered pewter plates. His bones shook with the impact but his inchoate wolfness rose to give his snarl a terrible menace. Both Marie and her grandmother staggered back, screaming, their mouths open in shock. Marie stumbled against a wooden stool, knocking it over.

The grandmother was the first to recover and pushed Marie in front of her. Bzou was outraged at such cowardice.

He glanced at the fireplace to his right because the harridan threatened to push Marie into it. The charcoal fire wasn't big enough to scare him. He feigned a move towards it. She threw Marie in that direction and rushed to her right on the way to the door. Good. If she left the cottage, then he could protect Marie. He growled deep and low, baring his teeth at the old woman to speed her exit then turned to the girl. More a young woman now. He calmed his face to reduce her fear.

How could he demonstrate that he was her childhood friend and not a wild animal? He lay down with his head on his paws, eyes doleful up at her, emitting the kind of whine canines have always used to endear themselves to humans. Sadly, her red, wet eyes remained wide open in fear.

He tried to say, 'Marie' but it must have sounded like an angry growl because she backed up, shaking.

He remembered a game they used to play. Bzou bit and held an apple from Marie's fallen basket then turned over onto his back. Hope willed her to recognize the inner being and for a moment he saw a glint, a narrowing of her eyes in understanding. At last, after all this time since the transformation, a karmic relief. Now, they could work on being together. A strange life, one of love conquering, controlling a numinous existence.

But her eyes changed to wide fear. Not *at* him but beyond.

He heard a creak from a floorboard. He leapt, taking him under the table just as an axe thudded into the floor where he'd been. His lupine instinct took hold, making him release a savage snarl. He scrambled away from the hag but realized she now possessed no weapon. He saw her scrawny ankles barely covered by ragged woollen socks. The wolf lunged and nipped at her feet. Her shriek hurt his ears but he was mistaken if he thought she would give up the fight.

Bzou needed to protect the girl yet fight the woman. He glanced over at Marie, who'd had the sense to cower behind a rocking chair. He'd wasted a second looking away from danger and it arrived on the side of his head. Scalding stew blinded his right eye. He turned to yelp in shock and dismay at his failure to rescue his sweetheart. Even so, he jumped in the grandmother's direction to prevent her regrouping, of finding more domestic weaponry. Too late, she'd armed herself with a poker, glowing cherry red at the end pointing at his charging face. He couldn't stop mid-flight but turned his head so it

141

was the pelt on his neck that singed, caught fire. More, a burning sensation as if the weapon was burying itself into his body. He now fell sideways onto the table, rolled and fell off the other side. A temporary respite but he couldn't believe how he was having such difficulty combating an ancient human like this. He would have been more successful as a young boy to get the girl out of danger. Grandmother might be old, but she was possessed, a succubus.

He backed up with the table between him and his quarry, his right eye unseeing, his left smarting. His fur smouldered. He saw red, but it was only Marie's cape she'd thrown over him to douse and comfort. Grateful though he was, he needed to shake it off and face their would-be killer.

Her voice, ancient and so wavering, faltering yet loaded with hate pierced through the remaining wisps of smoke and motes. She spat at Marie. "Rotkäppchen, you evil little bitch. I've known all along you only wanted to poison me with your baskets of food. I've never eaten none of it. Always put it out for *his* kind. Make *them* ill instead."

He assumed she meant wolves but she was mad enough to think all of forest kind were against her. Perhaps she was right.

"No more, missy. You and your pet won't live beyond today." The poker had cooled but it sported a cruel hook that could gouge an eye, a heart. Was she also going to hurl spells at them? Her expression with gapped toothy grin and lowered brow was now of easy confidence.

142

Bzou attempted to intimidate with fierce barking. Its staccato had the desired effect and she took a step back. She spat at him, as if that would make him surrender. He would never give in. His life's mission was to be the protector of Marie. Even at the cost of his life. Stop it, Bzou. He had to concentrate on the now, like the other wolves did. He should leap at the woman, risk being impaled on the poker and at the moment it wasn't pointed directly at him although that could be a ploy. She'd fall, during which he could bite at her neck, rip out her veins and windpipe. His real wolf compatriots wouldn't have been thinking this through. It would have been over by now. They wouldn't have broken in through the roof, nor stayed in the cottage to do battle. At most signs of resistance they'd run. Wolves only fight non-wolf animals to eat them, but the old woman wasn't on his menu. He was different on so many levels.

His introspection didn't reduce his growling and baring of yellow teeth. Frothy spittle dripped onto the floor, a phenomenon that surprised him, being not completely used to his body behaving without him asking it to. Even so, he was pleased with the effect of being bestial. His muscles and anger intimidated his adversary but it had yet to command a winning strategy. Should he really leap at her in spite of the poker that had already damaged him? He tensed his muscles ready for an attack when, too late, a brown blur passed him by and slammed into the old woman, sending her reeling backwards, banging hard into the rough wall.

Her scream pierced his ears, skull and heart so much he was silenced. The noise stopped.

The silence stunned him for a moment then although his vision remained blurred, he saw the grandmother bend her knees and sink a little. As hearing resumed, he detected laboured breathing, gasping. He smelt death stealing into the room. A chill ran through his veins.

He raised himself up on all fours to look for Marie. The chair she'd used as a shield rocked on its own. The girl wasn't there, but a green curtain rippled to the bedroom beyond. He looked back at Marie's grandmother. What had hit her and why was she partly stood against the wall, trembling so much?

His growl re-emerged as he approached her. He told his voice to still. So much instinct was a nuisance. He looked up at her face. Eyes open. Grey, bloodshot but dull, unseeing. Drool escaped from her mouth. Her arms hung limply down and she'd dropped the poker, which stuck upwards, lodged between two floorboards. Was it a ruse to lure him closer? He doubted she was pretending and nipped at her ankle again. No reaction, though he didn't like the texture of wool in his mouth. He reached up to her sleeve, closed his teeth around it and tugged a little then let go and stepped back in case she'd hidden a weapon up the other sleeve, waiting for the right moment. He barked to see if that shocked her eyes to open more. Nothing from her but he heard a movement to his right. He turned his head to look but the old woman lunged at him then so he leapt up at her only to find her falling on top of him, pinning him to the ground.

She was dead. It took a few moments for him to hunch his back and scrabble around to get free. Part of a deer antler was sticking out of her bloodied back. He looked up to see the rest of the broken trophy on the wall.

If he'd known as a child that the old woman could cast her evil magic on him perhaps he could have told someone in the village but even then the moment had passed. Was she protecting her granddaughter from the ordinary village boy or was she saving Marie for her own purposes?

Bzou heard a rustling again behind the curtain to the bedroom. He gave a short 'who's there' bark. A soft whine came back.

The curtain parted and a female wolf emerged. Blue, scared eyes. Marie.

The old hag had used that word on her, Rotkäppchen, it must have triggered a latent transformation. Were all local children prone to becoming wolves? Ah, the brown blur that flew past him at the old woman, who then staggered back and... He stepped out of Marie's line of sight so she could see the body. She came up and nuzzled him. They were together as children, now as wolves. Sooner or later the cottage would be entered by men and they'd assume the grandmother's killer was him or Marie or both.

Marie walked over the fireplace and tentatively put a paw towards it. Bzou understood. He pulled out glowing charcoal onto the rough straw mat.

145

Marie ran to the bedroom and returned with a thin bed sheet.

Soon a blaze sent smoke to the ceiling. They fed it with more clothing, wooden stools, an old book: her grimoire. She brought him her red cape. No, he didn't want that burnt. He leapt up at the door but it wouldn't open, until she stood on his back and lifted the latch with her paw. Outside, they stood, side by side, watching the building burn. She'd brought her cape outside, but really he knew it was impractical for her to keep carrying it. The cottage was hardly visible through the smoke. The thatch and even the living ivy caught fire with deep reds and orange flames. Purple smoke crackled into the air from potions. People would see the dense smoke, but such a sight and sweet aroma from charcoal piles were not unusual in the Wild Wood.

Even so, he heard a bark, then another. Not wolves but hounds. He feared for the inexperienced Marie. He left his urine markers on trees and made ready to lead them away. One more glance at the cottage as it crumbled and fell into its foundations.

***

They escaped through the trees. A last wistful look back at the forest, from which a thinning wisp of smoke was all that was left of the grandmother's wickedness. He looked beyond to the silver reflections of the moon in the river. Had he inherited the Bzou-ness from a human father or a wolf and did it need the old woman's spells to activate him as it did for Marie? Perhaps their future

in the forest beyond the mountains would have
fewer questions than answers than those in this
Eiger Wild Wood.

Arsenic and Red Leather

Jason R Frei

There once was a girl whose heart was wicked and selfish. She thought only of herself and of what others could do for her. Her raven black hair, snow white skin and ruby red lips made her the envy of all who beheld her. She wanted for nothing. Suitors from near and far gave her all that she desired.

Her most prized possession was a supple red leather-hooded cloak that her Granny gave to her when she was but a child. Its color shone like an apple fresh on the tree. Fur lined the interior of the cloak, making it warm and cozy. People marveled at its exquisite construction. The girl wore the cloak everywhere she went, so much so that people called her Red Riding Hood.

Red Riding Hood thought often of her cloak and how expensive it must be. She yearned for another of the same quality, but did not believe that her Granny would indulge in a second one. She fantasized of the riches that the old woman must have hidden in her cottage.

Her thoughts turned to obsession and she spent many a night dreaming of what she could do with so much money. So it was that Red Riding Hood hatched a plan to get rid of her Granny and inherit her immense wealth. She would poison her.

Red set about making a hearty meal for her Granny, who was old and frail. She added arsenic and belladonna to a bottle of wine as red as her cloak. She rubbed cyanide into a roasted leg of lamb. She crafted a mint jelly out of hemlock and white snakeroot. When Red finished, she packed the tainted meal into a picnic basket and went on her way.

Granny's house dwelt close to the other side of the forest. A dirt path wound through the woods. Posted signs warned travelers to keep on the path as wild and ferocious animals stalked through the forest. Red was also wild and ferocious and thought nothing of the animals that she may encounter.

As Red traveled on her way, she met a wolf who sat on a rock just off the path. He was a fine-looking specimen with a silver-gray coat and mischievous eyes. He was gaunt, but virile. Red, being the wicked girl she was, thought of the fun she and the wolf could have together. She approved of his lascivious smile and his musty scent directed tingles of pleasure through her body. Devilish and depraved thoughts ran through her head, but she remembered her plan and hurried past him.

The wolf was intrigued by this fearless girl. Something about her seemed familiar, but he couldn't quite place it. He smiled his handsomest smile, jumped lithely down from the rock and joined Red on the path.

"Good morning child," said the wolf. "Where are you off to in such a hurry this fine day?"

Red glanced sideways at the wolf with a crooked grin on her face. "I am on my way to see my Granny who is old and frail. I have meat and wine to help her get strength back in her bones."

The wolf smelled the wickedness in Red as it was in his nature as well. His fascination grew stronger as did his desire for the girl. He had to have her.

"Might I make a suggestion?" he asked graciously. "Do you see the sunbeams dancing in the light? Do you hear the birds singing their pretty little songs? You are yet a child and should take the time to enjoy what youth you have."

The wolf played not just on her youth, but on her sensibilities. "Perhaps gathering some flowers from yonder field will cheer your Granny up even faster?"

Red looked around her and marveled at the fields beyond the dirt path. A new plan took shape in her mind and her smile grew wider. She turned to the wolf.

"Thank you, kind sir. I shall pick her a wondrous bouquet of these beautiful flowers. I only hope that she does not wither away in my absence."

The wolf's smile grew wider. With Red busy, he could rush to Granny's house and take her place. He would wait for Red to arrive and take them both.

Why only eat mutton when I can have fresh veal as well? he thought.

He bowed deeply to Red and swept his arm out to the side. "If you would like, I could go watch over Granny and keep her company until you arrive."

Red turned on her charm and beamed at the wolf, giving him a small curtsy that showed a flash of her white thigh. "I would be so delighted. Her cottage is on the other side of these woods nestled beneath three large oak trees. Surely you know of where I mean?"

The wolf nodded and headed off down the path. Red climbed over the small fence by the road and made her way into the field. She looked once behind her to make sure the wolf had left and then lay down amongst the flowers. Her smile turned egregious and she thought to herself, *Perhaps the wolf will eat her before I arrive. Then I will be in the clear and her wealth will come to me naturally.*

The wolf made his way briskly to Granny's home. Thrice he circled the house inspecting it for traps. When he felt satisfied that all was safe, he peered through the dusty window that looked into the kitchen.

A hearth sat at the far wall with a fire burning inside. A large black cauldron sat over the fire, its insides roiling and bubbling. The wolf smelled an odd scent—one that was smoky and fatty with undertones both tarry and burnt. It reminded him of family and home. It made him nostalgic and uneasy.

A large wooden table sat in the middle of the kitchen. Meats and sausages spread out upon its marred surface. A large butcher's knife stood up from the corner that it stuck in. Blood congealed on the edges of the table and in a small gelatinous pool on the floor. Aside from the sparse furnishings, the kitchen appeared empty.

The wolf crept to the door and knocked softly.

"Who is there?" asked Granny.

The wolf cleared his throat and raised his voice. "It is I, Red Riding Hood and I have brought you food to mend you back to health."

151

"My dear child! I am too weak to get out of bed. Please lift the latch and let yourself in."

The wolf opened the door and stepped into the kitchen. The smell from the contents of the cauldron overpowered him. He looked over the room and noticed a small pile of skins behind the table. They ranged in color from reds to browns to silver-grays. Pointed bushy tails poked out from the heap. He realized at once that the furs were from wolves and the scent from the cauldron was of boiling leather. He crossed the room in a huff and dashed into the bedroom chamber.

Granny laid in bed with a thick blanket pulled up to her chin. Blue spider-veins criss-crossed her pale face. Two small black eyes peered out from a nest of wrinkles. A quilted cap perched on top of head. Thin, straw-colored wisps of hair peeked out from beneath.

The wolf fumed.

"I know you, woman!" His hackles raised and his lips drew back from his razor-sharp teeth.

He thrust a clawed finger at her. "You are the huntsman, the killer of wolves. Long have you stalked through these forests and taken my kin from me."

Granny said nothing, but cackled in a high-pitched keening voice.

The wolf pounced and struck her soundly in the head with the back of his brutish paw. She reeled, but remained conscious.

The wolf stripped her of her clothes. He bound and gagged her with thin strips of cord found discarded on the floor. He slavered and drooled over her exposed body. When he felt that her terror was at its highest peak, he stuffed her into the wardrobe next to the bed.

"You will watch as I rend and devour your grand-daughter, much like you have done to my kith and kin. I will pick my teeth with her bones and wear her skin like a cloak. When I am finished with her, I will take my time with you. You will know such exquisite pain as has never been felt before."

With that, the wolf closed the wardrobe. A gap stood between the doors allowing the frightened woman to see all that transpired in the room. The wolf dressed himself in her clothes and pulled the cap over his head to hide his ears and features. He lay in bed awaiting the arrival of Red Riding Hood. The bed was soft and warm and he soon fell asleep.

Red took her time wandering through the woods picking flowers for Granny. When she felt that enough time had passed for the wolf to do his deed, she went back to the path and continued on her way. The door to the cottage was open when she arrived. Red allowed a small giggle to escape. She composed herself and went inside.

Red stopped in the front room and called out. "Hello. Granny?"

The only response came from the cauldron still boiling above the fire. Red continued to the bedroom. She drew back the drapes on the four-post bed and saw her Granny dozing.

Red gently shook her. "Granny? I have come to feed you so that you may get better."

The wolf woke from his doze.

153

"My dear child," began the wolf. His voice was gruff and he cleared his throat several times. "I am very sick, grandchild. Perhaps some refreshment may do me well."

Red uncorked the wine and filled a glass. She put some of the roasted lamb on a plate.

"As you are so weak, let me feed you, Granny."

The wolf was ravenous as he had not eaten in some time. He allowed Red to feed him and he devoured the entire leg of lamb within minutes. The wine glass was filled and emptied many times over.

When he finished, the poison began to take its toll. The wolf struggled to breathe and his face contorted. His cap fell from his head.

Red saw the wolf in his true form. She took delight, thinking that the wolf had eaten Granny.

"Oh, Granny! What great ears you have!"

The wolf choked and could form no words. The wolf's eyes bulged in their sockets and tears streamed down his face.

"Oh, Granny! What great eyes you have!"

He opened his mouth wide and tried to inhale.

"Oh, Granny! What great teeth you have!"

Foam bubbled out from the wolf's lips and his tongue lolled in his mouth. Blood seeped and trickled down his nightgown. Red stood up and rejoiced. She danced around the bed as the wolf writhed in agony.

"You foolish wolf," she said as she danced. "I had come to kill my Granny and take her gold. Instead, you killed her for me and now you are done in by your own gluttony."

Red laughed and watched the wolf twist and squirm. He gave out one long hoarse howl and then collapsed, dead.

The wicked girl tucked the lifeless body of the wolf back into the bed and placed the cap over his ears. She took her time and rummaged through the small cottage looking for her Granny's riches. When she thought she had searched everywhere, her eyes lit on the heavy oak wardrobe. She crossed the small room to the dresser and threw the doors open in anticipation.

Granny leaped out with a large knife in her hand and drove the blade into Red's stomach all the way to the hilt. Red's eyes widened in surprise and she grasped her Granny's shoulders.

Granny looked deep into Red's eyes, pursed her lips and shook her head. She took out the knife and stabbed Red several more times.

"You came to kill me, granddaughter."

Red tried to shake her head no, but Granny placed her finger over the girl's mouth.

"Don't deny I, child. You never cared for anyone other than yourself. It was only a matter of time before you came for my wealth."

She laid the girl's body on the bed and turned back to the wardrobe. Granny heaved on a large trunk and pulled it out onto the floor. She opened the lid.

The chest was filled with gold coins, shiny gemstones and strands of pearls. Confusion crossed the sweat-slicked face of Red.

"An old woman living alone in the woods is bound to be set upon by thieves and brigands and others like them." She pointed to the bed. Where the wolf had been was now a silver haired man. "They provide me with wealth and... sustenance."

Granny smiled and her teeth were sharp and wicked. The last thing Red saw was her Granny's awful, jagged mouth opening wide around her head.

Lord of the Dance

Liam Spinage

I Danced In The Morning

They gather in their masses as he looks on from a nearby rooftop, restringing his violin and letting his bare feet dangle precariously over the edge to the packed streets below. Soon he will take his place at the head of the crowd and strike a tune, leading them on a merry procession through the city streets. For now, he appears content to watch the throng assemble in the main square; a panoply of masked and costumed partygoers, ready for a day of fun.

He stares down at them as one of them looks back and points up excitedly, nudging two of her friends and waving up at him from far below. He allows himself a polite wave and a bow, his fiddle flashing in the bright light of the morning sun. Then he withdraws from the edge to a small sack which contains his patchwork partywear and begins to climb into the voluminous robe.

On with the motley.

***

"I swear to you, that's him, look!" Sandra shielded her eyes against the sun and squinted back up at the figure on the rooftop. A serious young man next to her removed his mask and tried to match her line of sight.

"I can't see anything. Are you sure?"

"He's gone now, but he was there, I swear! That must be a good omen, to see him early! He even bowed at me!" Her companion side-eyed her sceptically then nudged the third of their group.

"Looks like the heat's got to Sandra already! Seeing things in the heat haze." He wiped matted black hair from his brow. "I'm going to keep my mask off until we start. It's way too hot to be wearing it already."

"That's bad luck." Sandra frowned, then looked dejectedly back at the roof.

"Y'know, I did see something. Maybe it was him. I've only seen a picture of him in the brochure though and whoever that was up there was wearing something quite different. But still..." Toby, the third of their party, craned his head again. Sandra smiled at him, glad to have a co-conspirator, even a half-hearted one. He snapped his head back. "Anyone fancy a beer? There's a little bar on the plaza a couple of roads over, we could chill there in the shade rather than sweat ourselves to death here."

"I told Libby we'd meet her here." Marcus looked around and shrugged. "Not that she'd be able to spot us in this madness at any rate."

Sandra didn't dwell on why Libby and Marcus hadn't arrived together, but did exchange a meaningful glance with Toby. *I hope everything's OK between them.* Toby shrugged in response. *I just wish he'd lighten up, it's supposed to be a party, for goodness sake.* "I'll text her. Come on. Let's see if

158

there are still places to sit down, there'll be plenty of time to stand up later."

***

Dance, then, wherever you may be -

His fingers were ever straying and impatient to be playing.

What lives have these people led? How empty must those lives be that they flock to this one particular place on this one particular day just to 'have fun'? Can merriment not be sought in other places, at other times? If people felt it necessary to have a season to be jolly, what did that say about their temperaments the rest of the time?

He knew this to be the case even as he rosined up his bow. He knew the indignities mankind inflicted on one another, hour after hour, day after day. It wasn't a surprise when you had been watching them, in one guise or another, for millennia.

Today he would lead them all away from this. Let them lose themselves in little moments of joy and ecstasy. Take them back to those rare and precious times, often in their childhood, when ignorance was bliss.

It wasn't that they deserved it, far from it. It was just what he did.

He opened up his case and said, "I'll start this show."

***

Sandra took one look at Libby as she approached and sighed audibly. Libby wound her way across the crowded plaza where the others sat at one of the trestle tables set up earlier that morning, under the shade of a giant yellow umbrella proudly emblazoned with the name of a beer none of them had ever heard of and were unlikely to drink if there weren't free samples given out to all the festival goers.

She tripped four or five times on her way to them, each time cursing the ground she walked on, her shoes, nearby patrons, whatever seemed appropriate. Sandra wondered whether she was incredibly hung over or still drunk and guessed this had been the source of the sourness she had detected with Marcus earlier. Whichever it was, it was going to cast a shadow over their whole day.

Libby waved hello as she spotted them and drew nearer. Her eyes were hidden behind mirrored sunglasses and the rest of her face was hidden in the shade of a wide brimmed bright yellow sun hat from the rear of which protruded a few stray blonde strands. She blew a kiss at a nearby waiter as she grabbed one of the promotional beers from the tray and sat down next to Marcus. Then she lit a cigarette and began to speak. Sandra could smell the tequila lingering on her breath from the night before.

"You left us early last night, Marcus! You missed the best bit of the party!"

Marcus squirmed his hand away as Libby attempted to grab it. Having failed, her limp wrist was left dangling over the side of the table, a golden bracelet flashing in the midday sun.

"Ooh, what happened?" Sandra was in no mood for this bullshit. Calling Libby out now was the best way to shut her up and a sullen, pouty Libby would be a better companion than the full-tilt party girl persona Libby liked to put on for an audience.

"Well, er, lots of stuff." Sandra smiled inside; as she thought, Libby had been too out of it to know. Probably still was. "Some of the musicians from the carnival joined us late, must have been about three in the morning. They played all night. All night, Marcus!" One last attempt at attention. It failed. Marcus had already withdrawn into the text of the festival brochure.

Libby downed her beer in one and then signalled for another. Sandra, after a moment's thought, did the same. If you can't beat them, join them.

***

I'll lead you all in the Dance

The procession snaked endlessly down Main Street, ebbing and flowing with the mass of sweaty flesh. He crooked his neck, just once, to check they were following him and flash them a knowing smile from beneath his quartered red and yellow mask. He pulled the strings across the bow and it gave an evil hiss. As it did, barely discernible wisps of yellow smoke began to issue from it and waft their way behind him into the madding crowd.

161

It hadn't always been the violin he'd used as an instrument of temptation, Far from it. Hundreds of years ago, the flute was the instrument of jollity he'd used to draw a crowd. He still carried that at his side; not in case the fiddle failed to enthral - it never had - but as a reminder of the power he had once wielded and the lessons humanity had yet to learn:

Always pay the piper.

Always give the devil his due.

Otherwise, all hell will break loose.

***

"I am *not* drunk!" Libby lashed out as Marcus tried to catch her, but promptly lost her balance and fell over sideways into a trash can. Sandra, surprising herself, erupted in fits of laughter. Marcus' face was a contorted mask of rage and frustration which had already progressed from '*you're embarrassing me*' to '*I'm not talking to you anymore.*' Toby just gazed stoically, arms folded, more annoyed that they were losing sight of the front of the parade where the musician was.

Since none of them seemed willing to help her up, Libby struggled to gain her own footing, managed on the third attempt. Sandra has stopped laughing by then but remained strangely mesmerised by her own choice of action not moments before. She held out a tanned forearm for Libby to grasp as she righted herself. Libby glowered crossly at her, refusing it, but changed her mind as she continued to wobble. She now reeked

162

of tequila and garbage though in Sandra's mind, Libby had always been garbage.

"Shall we?" Toby unfolded his arms and found a way for them through the closeness of the crowd, determined to have his fun that day, regardless of what the others did.

"Wait up!" Marco ran to him, out of breath even after a few paces. Sandra didn't hear what they said to each other as she was busy helping Libby divest herself of a few items of trash that had somehow made their way onto her ensemble. Still feeling puckish, she decided to leave the banana peel on her sun hat. Toby and Marco shared a brief laugh and then high-fived each other. Toby pulled something out of his shirt pocket which glinted briefly - *tin foil maybe? She wasn't really paying attention* - and they both took a pinch of something from it. Sandra sighed, reaching for her hip flask. Damned if she was going to be the only adult in the room yet again.

***

I am the Dance and I still go on

He turned a corner and led the merrymakers away from the main drag down toward the docks via a circuitous route through high-sided office blocks which then gave way to the warehouse district. There were less people watching from the doors and windows here but that wasn't important. Everyone he wanted had already joined the dance. They moved behind him as a mass of masked faces, each hiding their own thoughts, their own dreams.

He chose not to care what those were. Not this time. He wanted them to think as one, move as one, act as one. A single huddled orchestra for him to conduct. What to him if their cacophony was unmelodic, their speaking and shrieking and squeaking in fifty different sharps and flats? He was the Dance itself, the dance of life and death, and his tune carried throughout the aeons, a drum beat that pounded through history.

Around him, two circles of dancers began to writhe to his never-ending tune, finding their own rhythms in the procession. Others surged forward and formed one of these ever-expanding spirals which fanned out onto the promenade, the boardwalk, the docks and even some of the little jetties that jutted out into the quietly lapping water.

One circle moved slowly, clockwise, swaying slightly, their hands dipping and then rising in unison, prostrating themselves before him before picking themselves up. They fanned themselves out and began a gentle to-and-fro toward the rest of the approaching crowd. Their masks, every one, were sickly shades of yellow.

The other circle started slow but rapidly picked up speed. Theirs was not the languid rhythm of the yellow masks - their masks were deep hues of crimson and scarlet and they swayed frenetically from side to side, whirling like dervishes as they spun outwards.

Perfectly still, in the centre of the storm, the lord of the dance played on.

***

Libby hung over the iron railings which sealed the street from an alley full of broken bottles and broken dreams, retching repeatedly until her stomach was empty. Sandra looked on, no longer laughing but not caring either. Her eyes were glazed over and she looked longingly down at her empty hip flask. She began to feel ill both from the vodka she had drained and the awful reek of Libby's vomit which had completely ruined both their dresses. The guys were nowhere to be seen, not that either of them had noticed. She was about to say something to Libby when she heard screams begin to erupt from the crowd nearer the docks. Not the whooping and the hollering that had accompanied the procession, but full-throated shrieks of horror. She left the barely-conscious Libby behind and climbed a nearby fire escape to get a better view.

"We've lost the girls."

"Huh?" Marcus looked up from the brochure again and over at Toby. He squinted slightly - Toby seemed to be enveloped in a subtle swirl of sickly colours as flesh- and blood-hued wisps began to encircle him.

"I said, we've lost the girls." Toby looked worried. How long ago had they lost sight of them? Was it round the last corner? The crowd was pushing forward so quickly now and carrying them with it as the masses dispersed onto the waterfront. Toby wrenched the brochure from Marcus's hand and forced him to pay attention. "What is it with you and this brochure?"

"I've been trying to figure it out... the route we've taken is different to the one listed. Look…"

He grabbed the brochure back and opened it up full size to reveal the whole map. "We've gone down this way - Bedeil Street - rather than down Sarbarret." Marcus traced the new route on the map with his finger. He was alarmed to notice that he had pricked it somehow; there was a thin trickle of blood on the map. Then the map shuddered violently, distorting and contorting in his fingertips. Toby looked on in shock.

"Are… er... are you seeing what I'm seeing? It's… oh wow, it's beautiful."

Marcus wasn't seeing it at all any more. The blood had welled up behind his eyes and now flowed freely as he cried bright red tears. He clutched his face, dropped the map and fell to the floor.

"Whoah."

***

I am the life that'll never never die

His queer long coat from heel to head was half of yellow and half of red. He himself was tall and thin with sharp blue eyes each like a pin.

He smiled. He hadn't felt so alive since Hamelin.

That was him. The life of the party. Its pulse. Its heartblood. The Dance giveth and the Dance taketh away. Blessed be the Dance which creates and destroys both; which bringeth all things into being and finally undoes the illusion, releasing the souls of mankind from their purgatories of flesh.

And now for the finale.

***

"Marcus. Babes. Pick up." Libby could barely breathe let alone speak, but she'd managed one speed dial as she tried to climb over the railings to get away from the press of the crowd.

"Help, dammit!" She shook the phone in her hand as she was pushed back to the side of the street again when the throng surged past her once more.

"Hey! Watch what you're doing!"

"Libby!" She spun round, trying to find who had called her name. Her heart was beating fast now, her head spinning.

"Up here!"

Libby craned her neck, shielding her eyes against the sun. She had lost the shades and the hat somewhere around the third bout of vomiting. She could barely make out Sandra's shape three floors up, leaning against a fire escape and pointing excitedly up toward the waterfront.

"Get up here! I can see everything! Everything!" This last word was spoken slowly, tapering off into a distorted jangle of syllables Libby strained to understand.

"I know, Libby! I know!" Sandra's face, not that Libby could see it that clearly, was locked in beatific rapture. She tottered slightly as she tried to reach down to Libby three stories below.

167

"Sandy! Watch out!" Libby tried - far too late - to sober up, Sandra couldn't see everything, she reckoned. She couldn't see the strange vermillion clouds gathering overhead or the way the office blocks were slowly transforming into jagged sheets of humming crystal, Nevertheless, she tried to reach up - three stories wasn't that far, was it? It felt a lot closer than that - and then they would be able to connect again. The last she saw of Sandra was the look on her face when the ground shook beneath them, rocking the fire escape and sending her hurtling down, down, down with a look not of panic but serene beauty.

She took a long time to fall - much longer than Libby thought given that they were so close only a moment ago - their fingertips were nearly touching! Libby didn't have much time to react though, as the roaring crowd forced her body against a new growth of crystal shards which impaled her clean through. Her corpse twitched twice as the spiky crystal continued to grow through her. The crowd went wild.

Marcus pounded his fists hard against Toby's soft, yielding, flesh as he knelt over him on the street, letting the crowd trample over and past them. Toby was covered in his own blood now but still lay prone on the floor. The procession ignored them both, not that there was much of a carnival left - Marcus could just make out from his red-dimmed eyes that a number of similar fights seemed to have broken out. He turned his attention back to his prey and began to sink his teeth into Toby's shoulder as his hands reached down into Toby's shirt pocket where the little packets of yellow powder were still wrapped in their individual tin foil wraps. Marcus swallowed them all in one gulp, roared in triumph as he threw Toby's lifeless form to the baying mob and then pounced on another nearby partygoer, knocking him to the street and caving his skull in on the cobblestones. As the frenzied throng finished devouring his friend's body, the red clouds parted to a sickly yellow sky over a rugged landscape of crystalline formations towering forever upward.

The city and its people were no more.

***

I am the Lord Of the Dance

What next? Where next?

There is no what or where really, not to the Lord of the Dance. Nor a when. There is only one choice: What tune shall they dance to next?

Chains of Straw

Rie Sheridan Rose

I was happy at the mill. After Mother died birthing me, my life could have gone either way, but I was lucky. Father indulged me beyond all reason. I was his darling and could do no wrong. He bought me fashionable dresses and instilled in me a sense of entitlement I would have been better off without.

In return, as I grew, I became invaluable to his business. I learned to distract the eyes of the customers from the weights when it was time to pay for their flour—a pennyworth here, a half-weight there... it added up to bright, soft fabrics and sweets whenever I desired them. I like to think that I wasn't spoiled... but I am sure that was wishful thinking.

My father—ah, a bantam rooster of a man... heart as big as an ocean and a mouth to match. Especially when he'd tipped a few at the tavern. And he was at the tavern nightly.

So it was, on the eve of my eighteenth birthday, he opened his mouth a bit further than even he imagined. I heard about it from Pieter, the tap boy, the next day as he stole what he never realized would be his final kiss from me.

Father stood at the bar, one boot propped upon the rail, his cup never empty, but seldom full. "Here's to my lass, Belle!" he roared. "The prettiest girl in the kingdom, I'll warrant."

Few disputed that claim. I am not immodest when I say that I was always considered fair. If he had left his boasting with that claim, what followed would never have occurred... but someone scoffed. And Father never let a challenge lie.

"There are pretty girls wherever you turn," muttered the stranger. "What's so special about this Belle of yours?"

Bridling at the taunt, Father sputtered, "W-why...why, my Belle can spin straw into gold!"

I'm told the tavern went deathly silent. Those who knew my father's boastful ways made haste to try and get him in hand.

Pieter tried to laugh it off. "There you go again, Tobias, telling tall tales..."

But the stranger's imagination had seized the bait and did not wish to let it go. In the space of a moment, my world was turned inside out. And I wasn't even there to defend myself.

The next morning, Pieter was at my door almost before the sunrise to tell me the story. Even so, he beat the soldiers by mere moments.

I was bundled out of my comfortable home so quickly I had no time to grab a cloak and it was mid-winter. As I shivered between two silent guards, I begged the gentleman across from me to explain what was happening. I was alone and frightened—not my favorite birthday celebration for certain.

"You will be told everything you need to know when the time is appropriate," murmured the gentleman. I suppose he was trying to be kind, but it came across as mere indifference.

The carriage stopped in front of the castle that had dominated our village all my life. The high stone walls had always been fodder for stories and speculation, but none of us ever expected to actually step beneath that portcullis.

Now, I was hustled through the gate which towered over my head. The stones were ancient, moss-covered and cold.

I shook so as I walked beneath the arch that my guards were practically carrying me. I was dragged through halls filled with sumptuous furnishings and tapestries that still radiated bone-chilling cold.

I lost all sense of direction as we delved deeper and deeper into the bowels of the castle. Finally we stopped before a brace of thrones in an otherwise empty chamber. One of the seats was unoccupied— from the tracery of cobweb lace, for some time. The other held a man of darkness.

That was my impression of the king. It was not that he was dark—in fact, I've never seen a man so fair. His hair was like moonlight, his eyes so pale as to seem silver. His clothing was cream and gold, satin and brocade. Nothing about him was dark... and yet the whole felt black.

"This is the girl?" he asked and his voice too seemed lifeless and dark.

"Yes, Sire. The girl who spins straw to gold."

Pieter had managed to tell me Father's boast before the soldiers arrived, but I hadn't believed him. Surely no sane person would credit such nonsense. But the king was not sane, as I came to know.

"Excellent. Is the room prepared?"

"Aye."

"Excuse me," I ventured tentatively, trying to still my pounding heart, "prepared for what?"

The king turned his dead eyes upon me and I felt my soul shrink. "For you to spin, of course." He nodded at my guards. "Take her to the chamber."

"I don't know what you are talking about," I protested as they dragged me away.

"Better figure it out, dearie," said one grizzled soldier with a smirk. "The king's coffers are next to empty and if you can't fill them, he'll have no use for you—or your braggart father."

I might be able to appeal to the king on my own behalf—he was a man, after all—but I couldn't leave my father to his mercy. What was I to do?

They opened an iron-bound door set into thick stone walls. I was prodded through the opening into a stone-flagged room filled with straw. There was a spinning wheel before a three-legged stool. Other than that, there was straw. No bed, no facilities, just straw. It cascaded from the ceiling like a golden waterfall.

I sank upon the stool, staring at the straw. We were far below the surface of the earth. No light illumined the chamber except the torches in the corridor. Even if I had known how to spin, I would have had no light to do so.

The door shut behind me, the bar sliding to. A square of torchlight hit the spinning wheel. I stared at it helplessly... hopelessly. I could sit until the end of days and not be able to spin straw to gold. I could not even spin wool to yarn.

The straw filled the air with the smells of dust and sunshine. My mind drifted to the fields of summer...to the supple tanned boys with their bare chests bathed in sweat. To days of laughter and carefree flirtations. And I wept for days of beauty remembered. All alone with my thoughts and the memory of summer.

I don't know how long I sat, sobbing into my hands, before a susurration of sound impinged upon my consciousness. A light, scrabbling noise, as if a mouse was somewhere in the straw.

I wiped my hands upon my skirt, my eyes upon my sleeve. Curiosity has ever been my bane. "Who is there?" I whispered.

Like a mole breasting the earth, his head peeked forth from the mound of straw. And, where the king radiated dark despite his light coloring, he shone with inner light though his hair was black silk before his midnight eyes.

"I have come to ease your pain."

I choked on laughter. "Unless you can spin straw into gold, that seems unlikely."

His smile lit the room much more adequately than the torchlight. "Then it is a good thing I list that among my skills."

I stared at him.

He chuckled ruefully. "You don't believe me, do you?" he asked, his voice a whisper. "I suppose I must show you."

He held out his hand.

Hesitantly, I took it. He helped me to my feet, settled me into the straw and took my place on the stool.

His hands flew like lightning-winged birds, delicate and beautiful to watch. A twist of straw transformed to gold between his fingers and he fastened it about my ankle. "A token of faith," he murmured. "Believe me now?"

"But how?" I breathed.

"It is immaterial. The deed can be done. But...if I spin your straw to gold—save you from this dungeon cold... bring about your fate foretold—what, then, shall I get to hold?"

The words were formal, rhythmic, a charm, almost. I sensed that there was a hidden weight behind their pattern, even as he ducked his head with a wistful laugh and turned away. He was a twisted little slip of a man... with the eyes of a poet and a soul of fire.

I wracked my brains for an answer. I had been dragged away with little besides the clothes on my back, but upon the finger of my right hand I wore a simple band of silver won in a game of Forfeits from a field hand in the summer straw. I gave it to him willingly, small price to pay.

He took it with trembling fingers, breath caught between parted lips. He slipped it on his hand and began to spin.

***

I fell asleep somewhere in the night... lulled by the sound of the spinning wheel. When I awoke, it was to find myself curled on a thin pile of straw amid a shimmering sea of golden thread. I was alone—but not for long.

The door swung open and the cold king stood framed in the opening. He was a vision in white...but to me, he seemed a wraith, with dead eyes.

"Most impressive," he murmured, lifting a strand of gold from the pile. "You will do."

And he stepped back into the hallway and closed the door.

The guards came to remove the gold, bringing a bowl of soup and a crust of bread in exchange. A pitcher of water provided both drink and washing. The cell was bare to the walls except for the wheel, the stool, and me.

I searched it from top to bottom. There was no entrance beside the door. Where had my savior come from? Where had he gone? It hadn't been a dream—the chain about my ankle told me as much. But how could it have been real?

When next the door opened, the guards brought me a cloak—welcome in the cold, stone chamber—and escorted me to another cell. This chamber was twice the size of the first and stuffed without room to move with twice the straw as the previous day. The wheel and stool were wedged into the straw, a hollow scooped for me to sit within. I had to admire the king's persistence, although the gold already spun was worth a kingdom. His greed must know no bounds.

The guards shut the door without a word and I sat staring at the mountains of golden straw...wondering if he would come. I prayed he would.

I fell into an uneasy sleep. There was little else to do, since I was not the weaver. And in that sleep, I dreamt of a handsome prince—radiant in the sunlight—drifting past the mill in a gilded boat. He saw me at the window, and docked upon the shore, coming to me and brushing a kiss across my brow. He murmured "I love thee so..." in a voice like spring wine.

I gasped awake, bolting upright. And saw movement slipping into the shadows.

"Are you here?" I whispered.

"Yes."

I held out my hand and he took it.

Again, the formulaic words, "If I can break you from his hold, by spinning all this straw to gold—swell the kingdom's wealth tenfold—for what price is my labor sold?" There was something hidden behind those liquid eyes...swimming in their infinite depths...it almost broke the surface before it dove back into his heart.

I gave him a locket Father had said belonged to my mother, the only bit of vanity I had left and noted the silver band on his lily hand as he took it.

The straw transformed into gold so fast it seemed to melt. And as he spun, we spoke of inconsequential things, like dreams and joys... but nothing as monumental as names.

I almost soldiered through until morning, but at last, as the final wisps of gold were spun, I curled up in my cloak upon the floor...so did not see him go.

***

177

They say the third time is the charm. I suppose the king was fond of such old saws. The dungeon to which they hauled me next must have been a lower level, because it was double the width of the other cells and thrice the length. And I had never seen so much straw... not in a lifetime of milling. It packed the room so tightly that I was surprised there was room for me to sit. The wheel sat crookedly upon piles of straw. I was suffocating on the dust and fear. And yet, I prayed to see him. He was all I could think of. The gold, the king, none of it mattered. I would give him myself... as I had already given him my heart.

I turned—and he was there behind me, perched upon the heap of straw and watching with those eyes that gave away his secrets. I looked behind his twisted mask into the shelter of that hidden heart, and all the walls came crashing down.

He held out his hand and I took it. The charm sprang from his lips, "Here we are, as was of old— you with straw that must be gold—I, with hands the secret hold—what gift shall I now be doled?" The words were soft, and oh... so infinitely sweet.

"Whatever you desire," I whispered back. I went to him with the only thing I had left—starting with a kiss. From my soul to his.

And his hands spun so fast that the gold flowed like a river, washing me to a throne.

***

The king insisted on a formal wedding. He was not about to let go of a prize of such potential. I hated him as much as I loved the other...but I had no choice. My love had told me so.

At least the cobwebs have been brushed from my throne... but as my belly swells, my heart shrinks. I both fear and crave this child. The child I know will be darkly light, instead of golden dark.

While I still can, I run the chain around my ankle through my fingers... and I wish I knew his name.

Little Red Cyber Head

Gary Budgen

They called her Red. At that moment her skin
was scarlet, the colour of old British soldiers. She
leant against the plate-glass window of the pet store,
using their network to make a connection. By the
time the owner, Bob, realized what she was doing
and came out to shoo her away she would have had
plenty of pseudo-time to navigate through
cyberspace and check on Granny.

The familiar data landscape was made up of
networks that looked like solid blocks if, secure, or
odd amalgamations of shapes were left open
without security. Her avatar was her own, now
enthusiastically carmine coloured, floating head. It
sped onwards. When she got to the sanatorium the
system recognized her as a next-of-kin, letting her
settle in the virtual vestibule. One of the staff, a
generic nurse-face, appeared.

"Ah, Ms. Hood," it said, "your grandmother is
in the down cycle at the moment."

"Just thought I'd check in."

The scene faded out and Red navigated through
the system to the CCTV in Granny's cubicle.
Granny was there, asleep and breathing contentedly.
It would be another week or so before they would
wake her from the induced slumber for her day of
up time. Granny's avatar would be in the rest room
so Red went there.

The rest room was a mock-up of geometric shapes trying to be furniture, cheap rendering. Usually there would be a bunch of avatars of the sleeping residents here but as Red came in she saw these, and Granny too, only momentarily. They all turned to look at her and began to transform, merging into a single shape, the eyes glowing red, the jaw becoming elongated and sprouting vicious teeth. The giant wolf head swooped towards Red and even before reaching her Red could feel it attempting to breach her avatar, to wound her psyche.

Red cut out.

She was outside the pet shop, slumped on the floor. She had vomited onto the ground. The world spun round and she tried to focus on the large form looming over her.

"You all right?" said Bob, "You don't look so good. You gone all pinkish."

Bob sat her on a chair behind the counter and bought her a cup of strong, sweet, tea. The pet shop had a row of shelving dividing it into two aisles, dog and cat food, bags of grain and pet toys. Along each wall were vivariums and cages. There was an ancient bull-terrier asleep in a basket and a buddle of kittens curled around each other in a box in the corner.

Red sipped her tea.

Down one of the aisles came a creature like nothing she had ever seen before. It was the size of an obese cat with a spiky mane of dark grey that might be scales. It plodded slowly towards the counter.

"What happened to you?" said Bob. "I come out to tick you off for using my network, again, and you look like you're about to keel over. Your colour's only coming back now."

"Something's happened to my Granny."

"Anything I can do?"

"I think I'm going to have to go over there."

The scaled creature came and sat at Red's feet. It was not quite a lizard.

"Where?"

"Abeltown."

"That's right across the city. You'll have to take the loop."

"Quicker through the forest."

"Well good luck with that."

The creature at her feet snuggled closer to Red.

"He likes you," said Bob.

"What is he?"

"Called a Mark 6 Guardian. I call him Blinky. They make them in labs. I don't normally keep anything like that but I got him from a rescue centre. He's not for sale. I think maybe they use them in military zones and the like."

"What good would he be in a military zone?"

"Well, they reckon Guardians can be pretty vicious. Plus, he does have a pretty nifty defence."

"What do you mean?"

"Watch him."

Red looked down at the Blinky.

"I only found out by accident," said Bob. "I dropped a whole crate of cat food while he was just in front of me…. I don't like to scare him, though, so I trained him. Go dark, boy, go dark."

The creature vanished.

"What?" said Red.

Bob got some cat crunchies from a shelf and scattered them on the floor.

"Come back now."

The creature reappeared and began to eat. Bob scratched him behind the ear.

"Well," said Red, "I'm glad his enjoying a happy retirement. How does he do that trick?"

"Well," said Bob, "I'm guessing it isn't a million miles from the way your skin changes colour. You have a layer of guanine crystals under your skin, yeah, and they respond to your moods or whatever by changing their configuration and that alters the wavelength of light being reflected. I guess the military have taken it to a whole new level."

The creature finished its crunchies and came back to sit at Red's feet.

"Well," said Red, "I'd better be going."

"You take care in that forest," said Bob.

"Sure."

Blinky followed her to the door with Bob and they both stood on the porch to watch her go. When Red turned back to wave she saw the creature vanish before her eyes once more. Perhaps he didn't much like the outside world.

***

The city's river ran in a deep concrete culvert with a towpath on either side. It went through the neighbourhood. Red went down metal steps that creaked and wobbled. The river stank. It was coated in dark pond weed so that in places it had become almost stagnant. Plastic debris floated on it. Still, it was the quickest way to where she was going. The forest.

The river passed through a district of obsolete industrial units, their smokestacks and derricks seeming even taller that they were from the depths of the river culvert. Eventually she emerged into open ground as the river entered the forest ahead. The trees spread before her.

Some effort had gone in to the work. The trees were different sizes and shapes, had variations of leaf patterns and had been planted according to a carefully worked-out algorithm. Still they didn't look quite like real trees and, Red supposed, that if she ever did see a real forest it wouldn't be really like this.

The ground was coated with a chalky residue that fell from the artificial sodium-carbonate coated leaves super-efficiently sucking greenhouse gases out of the air. Much better than real trees. It had all been part of the renewal projects from years ago. The whole thing had been so popular that people had come to love the place, walking here, enjoying the tranquillity. Those days were long gone.

Once she had entered beneath the boughs, the sunlight became a patchwork on the ground, light in places, picking out the years of ground-in footprints in the compacted chalk.

There were no official paths, just endlessly splitting desire lines made years ago. Red would keep the river to her left, sighting it through the trees as she progressed. The idea was to get through the forest as quickly as possible. To go unnoticed.

It wasn't long, though, before something was pawing at her interfaces.

"Little girl," a soft voice cooed.

Red quickened her pace, scuffing up chalk flakes.

"Little girl."

Images began as colours in her peripheral vision. The trouble was, if she carried on trying to ignore it then it might try a direct assault. So she stopped and sat down with her back against a tree. She dropped into pseudo-time onto whatever local network was being used to try and contact her.

The avatar was the face of a woman with grey hair in dreadlocks.

"What do you want?" Red's virtual head asked.

"I was wondering what you are doing here, little girl. This is a dangerous place."

"I know. The gangs. That's why I'm trying to get through as quickly as possible."

"Yes, yes. You must be careful. The gangs. This used to be such a wonderful place. That's why I chose it when I died. I thought my avatar could wander blissfully through the network here forever. But the world moves on."

"Just like I should."

"Oh yes, I mustn't keep you. It's just so nice to talk to someone. Why are you here? Where are you going?"

The avatar grew close to Red's own. The woman must have had a kindly face in life. She was rendered here with bright eyes and a smile made of gentle wrinkles.

"I'm visiting my Granny."

"That's good. That's very good. Why don't you tell me all about her?"

Something was disturbing pseudo-time, a sensation pressing against a part of her body. She cut the connection.

"What the...?"

Blinky was sat at her feet. She saw the tracks he had made across the chalky ground.

"You gave me a fright," she said, "What did you do? Follow me from Bob's? Well, I'm not going back now. You'll have to come with me."

She began to jog, the creature keeping up with her. She ignored the voice calling, little girl, little girl, stay and talk, until at last it faded away.

At some point she lost sight of the river, gone beyond thick artificial trees that had become overgrown with natural vines and an undergrowth of woody scrubs. Maybe the river was behind all that. If she just kept going in the same direction she would be all right. But soon the thickets of shrubs blocked her way.

"Looks like we're stuck," she told Blinky.

The creature looked up at her for a moment, then shuffled forward a bit. It stopped at the undergrowth and sat up on hind legs.

"I guess we'll have to double back."

With a snick, claws sprung out of Blinky's paws. In rapid motion it began thrashing at the branches of the shrubs. Red came over and joined in, pulling away as best she could. In a few minutes they'd cleared a path through. They emerged back into an area of the artificial trees. The muddy bank of the river was just ahead.

"Girl. Girl."

It was a real voice. Harsh, sneering.

Soon others joined in.

"Girl. Girl."

"Watch her flesh grow redder," someone said. Someone too close.

She turned back into the forest but the voices were all around.

"Girl. Red Girl."

She began to run, back the way she had just come. But when she reached where the trees were sparse again they were waiting for her. Kids really. Raggedly dressed but still managing to effect some kind of gang identity with bandanas and neckerchiefs of blue.

Two boys and a girl ahead. Red could hear others all around.

"What do you want?" Red said. Trying to sound confident.

"Girl," said one of the boys, lanky kid with fair hair, blade in this hands. He took a few steps forward. Around her the forest was alive with movement.

"Girl," he said again.

Others echoed the word. A chant through the forest.

He laughed and came at her, slashing the air back and forth. The others were laughing. There seemed to be absence of awareness in them. Replaced by a mania.

187

Blinky vanished and Red turned to run, but there were others behind her. She balled her hands into fists. There was only one thing to do.

"Little girl." A different voice. The voice of the old lady, threatening to drag her into pseudo-time. "Little girl. Little girl." The voice became gravelly. Then growled.

"Not now."

The kid with the knife sprang at her and then began to scream with pain, thrashing around as his face became slashed and bloody. He fell to the ground. Red ran through the nearest gap. Behind her others were crying out in agony too.

She ran on, soon aware that something was following her. She looked back to see the wake it was causing. The dust stirred up, branches were breaking. It was only when she began to flag and turned at last to face it that Blinky suddenly chose to shed his invisibility. He bound towards her, mouth and claws caked in blood.

They went on after Red rested for a minute. She'd lost the sense of where the river was but finally they emerged from the forest and she could get her bearings. This was a largely abandoned part of the city with boarded up shops and houses and then a zone of warehouses. Granny's sanatorium was here, one among many. The interest on Granny's meagre savings meant she could only afford the Basic Low Care Package. She was kept in induced sleep to be woken once a month, but with an avatar free to roam the rest of the time.

As Red approached, the nurse-face avatar tugged at her interfaces and Red dropped into pseudo-time.

"Ms. Hood. I'm afraid that due to an ongoing emergency we are not able to accept visitors today. Please try again."

"I want to see my Granny."

"I'm afraid…"

The nurse glitched, flashing in and out of existence.

"I'm afraid… I'm afraid…"

Then disappeared entirely. Red went back into real time.

Red, with Blinky at her side, strode towards the entrance, a reception block tacked onto the front of the building. As she did a retractable metal shutter began to fall. Other shutters came down across the windows. The sanatorium had been sealed.

"Little girl. It seems your trip has been wasted."

Pulled back in pseudo-time Red saw it was the avatar of the old woman from the forest. Red's own head avatar faced her.

"What are you doing here?" Red asked.

"Oh. I live here. At least I did live here. I suppose part of me still does. But I can go anywhere now. I can be anything now."

"I thought you were part of the forest network."

"Oh I'm that too. Don't you get it yet?"

The avatar changed turning into the face of an old man, a succession of others, older men and women, a nurse, and finally assuming her granny's face.

"Do you like this one?" the avatar said.

189

"You're not Granny."

"No. Well part of me is. I've taken all of them. The processing power of all the avatars here, then the ones out in the forest. All the kids there worship me. I think of them as my cubs. It wasn't very nice what your pet did to them."

The avatar changed again, face stretching, ears growing, then sprouting the fur and fangs of a wolf.

"What are you?" said Red, "This is just another mask."

"Ah, if it were that simple," said the wolf, "No, but I am not that simple. Two avatars colliding, corrupting each other, absorbing the resources of each other. Then of more and more avatars. Soon I'll move on to the next sanatorium, then the next."

The onslaught was vicious, the wolf merging into Red's avatar, trying to infiltrate her local memory cache, subroutines and then connective software that interfaced with Red's brain. Soon Red would be completely overcome, annexed into this great multiple person thing, this wolf.

Searing pain cut through everything. She was out of pseudo-time, lying on the ground. Blood was pumping from her hand where Blinky had bitten her.

The pain was good. It focused her in the real here, the real now. She bound her hand quickly with a ripped sleeve from her shirt.

"Blinky," she said, "Do you think you can get me in there?"

The creature looked up at her. She stumbled over to the shuttered reception door and banged on the metal.

"I need to get in," she said. "You think you could do that?"

Blinky's claws snicked out again and slashed long cuts in the metal. It was cheap stuff. Good enough to keep junkies out if they came for the drugs but not a military Guardian it seemed.

"Little girl," the voice growled and Red focused on the pain in her hand, the throbbing through her nervous system. She climbed through the hole Blinky had made, the creature jumping through after her. A nurse was slanted over the desk in Reception. He was twitching, lost somewhere in pseudo-time. Red lifted his head and slapped his cheek. His eyes opened, flickered and he tried to slump again. Red slapped him harder until at last he woke properly, vomiting over the counter.

"You need to wake everyone up," she told him.

"What? I can't. They're never awake all at the same time. That's the whole point of the Basic Low Care Package."

"Just do it. Whatever's attacking this place is using them."

A growl came. "Little girl. You'll kill me if you do."

Red dug her finger into the cut in her hand, savouring the spike in pain.

The nurse was closing his eyes. She slapped him once more.

"Just do it."

***

191

She walked through the sanatorium past the cubicles she saw them all stirring, faces familiar from when the wolf had used them. When she reached Granny's cubicle she found the old woman sitting up in bed. The quizzical look on her face was replaced by a smile on seeing Red.

"You've come to see me properly. How lovely. And you a beautiful shade of coral today. And who have you got with you? Is that your dog? I haven't seen a dog like that before."

"His name is Blinky. He's my friend. How are you, Granny?"

"Oh, I'm fine. I think. But I've been having the strangest dreams."

"I'll bet. You know I think there's too much sleeping going on around here. I think maybe it's time you came and lived with me."

They would go back on the loop this time. Take Blinky back to Bob, who was probably worried about the creature.

"Yes, I'm taking you out of here, Granny."

Granny smiled again. Red listened to all her objections, about the cost, about how it would be a burden, how it wasn't too bad here after all. But in the end she relented.

"Perhaps you're right," said Granny. "Those dreams were getting strange. But you know, it wasn't all bad being a wolf."

Collector of Teeth

Travis Mushanski

"What the heck are you reading?"

Victoria chuckled and turned the National Inquirer magazine towards her husband. Her cheeks turned red and she averted her eyes from his judging gaze. "I just can't help myself."

"You know this is just trash, right?" Jason shook his head and sat next to his wife on the couch. "They're literally making up nonsense to take your money."

"I know, I know," Victoria admitted it. "But when Ava and I were in the check-out line today, the headline jumped out at me."

Jason dragged out the silence as long as he could before his wife's widening eyes and smile made him take the bait. He slumped back into the couch and said, "Okay, fine. What was the story?"

"Get this!" Victoria sat up straight and proud. "There's a new serial killer in our very own state. Already half a dozen victims."

"Oh, great." Jason smiled and then teased, "is it a wolf-man, alien or your average run of the mill swamp-thing?"

"Oh, shut up." She playfully smacked Jason's shoulder. "The thing is this killer doesn't actually kill. He steals his victims' teeth."

"Babe," Jason coughed to suppress a burst of laughter. "I admit it's a gruesome thought, but if this was true, wouldn't you think I'd have heard about it at work?"

"Well, Babe," she mockingly put air quotes around the word. "You aren't really on the front lines at the hospital. You're a psychologist who works in rehab. Just happens to be the same building."

"Ya, well, we do talk to other departments." He shifted away from his wife.

"So, what you're saying is, you wouldn't mind sending out a text or two for your beautiful wife." A mischievous grin formed on her face as she slid closer to her husband. "Maybe it'll help calm my nerves." She nestled herself into her husband and kissed his neck. "Maybe then I can calm your-"

"Momma, look!" Ava came bouncing into the living room with an enormous smile. "I got a wiggly tooth. I got a wiggly tooth!"

"Oh wow, honey." She twisted herself off Jason and gave him a coy smile followed by a slap on the thigh. "That's super exciting. Come show mommy and daddy."

"It's the top one," Ava declared while opening her mouth as wide as she could get it.

Victoria gently prodded the girl's upper incisor teeth. The one on the right was indeed loose. "Yep. You got a loose tooth right there."

"Does this mean I won't be a vampire anymore?" Ava frowned and dipped her chin to her chest.

"Pardon me?" Jason's eyebrow raised as he cocked his head to his wife.

194

"Honey," Victoria said softly to her daughter. "That was supposed to be our little secret."

"Wait a second." Jason shook his head in disbelief. "Did mom say you look like a vampire because of your two big girl teeth?"

"Sorry, momma." She started to sniffle, which meant tears were on their way.

"Don't get upset, Ava." Victoria wrapped her hands around her daughter's shoulders. "Dad's just being a grump. Why don't you show him how you pretend to be a vampire?"

Ava stepped back from her mother's embrace and stumbled towards her father with a devilish smirk on her face. She stretched back her upper lip to expose two canine teeth noticeably larger than her other baby teeth and lunged towards Jason, making a loud hiss. He jumped off the couch, pretending to be scared of the child vampire. When Ava made her final attack, he scooper her up and gave her raspberries on the neck until they both fell to the floor laughing.

"Okay, goofs." Victoria grinned as she stood Ava up. "It's time for all little vampires to go to bed." Ava groaned as she was ushered down the hallway to her bedroom. "And don't forget to brush those teeth, missy."

"Is Daddy gonna come too?" Ava whined as she trudged to the bathroom.

"Daddy just has to do something quick for mom before he comes to bed." She glanced over her shoulder and winked at Jason who nodded in return.

Jason fell backwards into the couch, kicked his feet up on the opposite arm rest and then reached blindly over his shoulder to grab his cell phone off the end table. He swiped though his cell phone apps, but when he got to the text message screen, his mind drew a blank. He knew people in other departments at Saint Andrews Hospital, but who would take him serious long enough to waste their time on something so foolish. *I can't believe I'm even going to attempt this*, Jason thought as he tapped the phone against his forehead.

He scanned through his contact list and selected the name Greg Higgens. Greg worked as a nurse at Saint Andrews, and after meeting via various patients, the pair's casual meetings grew into friendship. *I hope this doesn't push the friend boundaries too much,* he thought as he typed messages:

Jason: hey Greg! Sorry for the late text, but the wife is sending me down the rabbit hole. See anyone come through there with missing teeth?

Jason: no rush. Cheers!

He swiped through his contact list as he waited for Greg's reply, but when he came across Nancy Cartwright's name, he immediately mashed the phone icon to place the call. *Come on Nancy, you work-a-holic, please tell me you're still at work!*

After a few rings, Nancy answered the call with a peppy, "Hey, Jason. What did I do to deserve such an honour?"

Jason fist bumped the air and chuckled into the receiver. "Nice to hear your sweet voice too,

Nancy." He paused to scratch his head before dropping the nonsense into her lap. "Listen . . . I'm just doing some reconnaissance for Victoria."

"Oh, no. Is she back on the tabloid train again?" She laughed into the receiver and added, "Lay it on me."

"Looking for people admitted with teeth forcibly removed."

"Sounds gruesome," Nancy responded with the nonchalance of someone working in the medical field. "Listen, I'll check the database and let you know. May take a while, but I'll see if anything turns up."

"That's why you're my favorite hospital administrator."

"Nice try. You know you owe me one this time," she playfully lectured. "I'll let you know, when I know." Nancy abruptly ended the call, and Jason tossed the phone back onto the end table.

"You coming, Daddy?" a faint voice echoed through the house. "I'm all ready for bed."

"Be right there, my little vampire." He flipped off the lights as he made his way to his daughter's bedroom.

***

Jason's cell phone flashed to life shortly after midnight. It vibrated on the end-table before it went to voicemail. There was an abrupt vibration implying that the caller, Nancy Cartwright, had left a voicemail.

197

Thirty minutes later, the phone vibrated three times in short succession, displaying Greg Higgens' name. Three messages scrolled across the face of the touchscreen phone before the device reverted back to black. The messages read:

Greg: Sorry, dude. Been a crazy night.

Greg: A couple just rolled into ER. Drugged. All teeth missing!

Greg: Picked up in Hillsdale. Isn't that your neighbourhood?

***

A tug at Jason's pajama pants pulled him out of the dream world. A sense of dread washed over him as he slid into the world of the living.

"Daddy?"

He groaned and asked, "You okay, Ava?" He patted the blankets next to him where his wife was still fast asleep. She snored softly but didn't stir at his touch. "Did you have a bad dream, honey?"

"The tooth fairy came," she squealed.

"Oh, that's awesome," he feigned excitement. Jason knew she had a loose tooth, but couldn't remember one missing before bed. "Did she give you something good for it?"

"The tooth fairy is a boy, Dad," his daughter lectured. "But he did give me one of these gold coins." An object slipped into Jason's hand. It felt about the size of a Canadian dollar but quite a bit heavier.

198

Jason rolled over and flipped on his bedside lamp. The sudden blast of light was blinding, but he examined the coin through slitted eyes. It was one inch in diameter by a quarter inch thick, and to Jason's astonishment, it appeared to be made of solid gold. *The damn thing shimmers like sunshine,* he thought. On one side of the coin was a faded impression of a man encompassed by the word 'Liberty', and the other was stamped with the Great Seal of the United States. He bit into the piece like an old prospector. When the coin broke in half, Jason realized it was only chocolate wrapped in gold foil.

"Honey, why did you say the Tooth Fairy was a boy?" He looked up and froze before he could say anything else.

The lamp's light highlighted a trail of dried blood plastered across her cheek. He hadn't noticed it in the darkness, but he saw it clearly now. Her smile stretched ear to ear and revealed a noticeable void where her two eyeteeth should have been.

"Oh my god, Ava!" Jason hauled her into an embrace. He wiped the crusted blood off her cheek and pulled up her upper lip to inspect her mouth. The craters that once housed her vampire teeth pulsed with congealed blood. "What happened? Those were your new adult teeth. Who did this?"

Ava rolled her eyes and sighed. "Dad, I already told you!" She explained while making a sweeping gesture towards the bedroom door. "The Tooth Fairy."

Jason squinted to see past his daughter into the darkness of the room. The light from the lamp didn't penetrate deep enough to see through the open bedroom door. The blackness in the doorway shifted. Jason scuttled back against the headboard as a refrigerator-shaped figure filled the doorway.

The lamplight illuminated the shadow figure as it stepped into the room. A blood-stained lab coat hid its monstrous bulk. The floorboards squeaked beneath the man's girth as he adjusted his weight from one foot to the next. He thumbed a pair of wet pliers in one hand and gripped a cylinder connected to a gas mask in the other. His square, expressionless face stared down at the family through a pair of leather aviator goggles.

"Holy shit! Victoria! Wake up!" He shook her violently until her body rolled over. Her anesthetized eyes rolled back into their sockets and her mouth fell open into a gaping, toothless smile. A mixture of drool and blood pooled on her pillow.

A firm hand lifted Jason like a child and pinned him to the bed. He kicked and flung his arms about in desperation, but he couldn't remove the mountain bearing down on his chest. He wanted to scream, but he couldn't even breathe. His vision blurred as he lost himself in the Tooth Fairy's magnified eyes.

The pressure was released from Jason's chest moments before he lost consciousness. He instinctively sucked in air to fill his lungs but quickly perceived the strange aroma of permanent markers. A sly smile formed on the Tooth Fairy's face showing off two perfect rows of pearly white teeth. In the reflection of the aviator glasses, Jason could see himself breathing out of the facemask.

"Just breathe in deep, Daddy." Ava's voice came through over the growing cloudiness of anesthesia. "He promised to leave you gold coins under your pillow like he did for Mommy." A tiny hand tightly grasped his own to provide support.

All fear, anxiety and panic left Jason's body as the anesthesia took hold. His entire being floated on a cloud of feather pillows. The facemask slid off as the Tooth Fairy reached for a pair of stainless-steel pliers. Moments before Jason's eyes dropped shut to embrace unconsciousness, he noticed a pair of sparkling purple fairy wings attached to the Tooth Fairy's back. A warming sense of child-like whimsy pulled him back into the world of dreams.

Meet the authors

Dan Allen is Canadian and enjoys spending time in Northern Ontario. You can find his short stories in numerous magazines, anthologies, and podcasts. Visit www.danallenhorror.com to see a presentation of his published work.

His terrifying look at Alzheimer's, "Above the Ceiling," is featured in Bards and Sages collection of the Best Indie Speculative Fiction Vol. 2.

A personal favourite, "Sympathy for the Zingara," can be found in the March 2019 edition of ParAbnormal Magazine.

His terrifying story, "The Basement" (edited by Horror Zine's Jeani Rector), was published by Hellbound Books in July 2020.

You can visit Dan at www.danallenhorror.com and follow him on Facebook and Twitter at

@danallenhorror. You can write to Dan at contact@danallenhorror.com

Gary Budgen lives and works in London. His previous work has appeared in various magazines including Interzone, BFS Horizons, Morpheus Tales, Sein und Werden and the BFS Award short-listed anthology Humanagerie from Eibonvale. His work has been in many other anthologies from publishers including Thirteen O'Clock Press, Boo Books and Horrified Press. A collection of stories, Chrysalis, is published by Horrified Press and the chapbook Fragments of Onyx by Salo Press. A full publishing history can be found at garybudgen.wordpress.com.

Gina Easton is a former registered nurse who decided to pursue her long-time dream of writing as a profession. Since starting her new career in 2019, she has had fourteen short-stories published in horror anthologies and magazines.

Her debut horror novel, Black Jack, was released by World Castle Publishing in late December 2020. A second novel, a supernatural romance, is due out in the summer of 2021.

She adores the weird, mysterious and magical aspects of life, which she explores through her writing. She lives in Toronto, Canada, with her husband.

Jason R Frei lives in Eastern Pennsylvania where he works as a therapist with children and adolescents. He writes speculative fiction culled from the experiences of his life and those he works with and blends science fiction, fantasy and horror into new creations. His flash story "The Garden" will be featured in the horror anthology 99 Tiny Terrors by Pulse Publishing and his short story "Some of the Parts" will be featured in the horror anthology Toilet Zone 3: The Royal Flush by Hellbound Books Publishing. Visit him online: https://facebook.com/odinstones.

Brooke MacKenzie is a scary movie fanatic and writes horror fiction by candlelight. Her first book, Ghost Games, will be published later in 2021 by Dreaming Big Publications. She received a B.A. from Sarah Lawrence College and an Ed.M. from the Harvard Graduate School of Education. Her writing has appeared in several places, including *Who Knocks? Magazine* and *The Dead Games: A Zimbell House Anthology*. She is the current Board Chair of the New York Writers Coalition, which is the largest community-based writing organization in the country. She lives in Northern California with her husband and daughter. Visit her website: bamackenzie.com

Geoff Nelder lives in Manchester with his physicist wife, cycling rural lanes for thinking time. Geoff is a former teacher, now an editor, writer and fiction competition judge. His novels include historical fantasy Vengeance Island; Scifi: *Alien Exit*; *The ARIA trilogy*; The vegan scifi *Flying Crooked* series with *Suppose We* released 2019 followed by *Falling Up*; *Kepler's Son* and *Vanished Earth* on the way. Thrillers: *Escaping Reality*, and *Hot Air*. Collection: *Incremental*– 25 surreal tales more mental than incremental. Non-fiction includes climate books relating to his urban microclimate research, winning him a Fellowship of the Royal Meteorological Society. Geoff's website: https://geoffnelder.com

Aaron Padley says: With a horror obsession since childhood, and a passion for writing, it was only a matter of time before he delved into the genre himself. Ever the introvert, he spends all of his time either writing or hiking through the Lake

District, his home, for inspiration. As a relative newcomer to writing, his future is dark, but as any horror fan will tell you, that's how it ought to be.

Rie Sheridan Rose multitasks. A lot. Her short stories appear in numerous anthologies, including Killing It Softly Vol. 1 & 2, Hides the Dark Tower, Dark Divinations, and On Fire. She has authored twelve novels, six poetry chapbooks, and lyrics for dozens of songs. She is also editor-in-chief for Mocha Memoirs Press and editor for the Thirteen O' Clock imprint of Horrified Press. She tweets as @RieSheridanRose.

Liam A Spinage is a former philosophy student, former archaeology educator and former police clerk who spends most of his spare time on the beach gazing up at the sky and across the sea while his imagination runs riot.

David Turnbull is a member of the Clockhouse London group of genre writers. He writes mainly short fiction and has had numerous short stories published in magazines and anthologies. His stories have previously been featured at Liars League London events and read at other live events such as Solstice Shorts and Virtual Futures. He was born in Scotland, but now lives in the Catford area of London. He can be found at www.tumsh.co.uk.

Stuart Holland is the owner of Fiction4All, a golf enthusiast (especially the 19th hole) and has written in the genres of crime/mystery, thrillers and suspense and has now turned his hand to horror. His books are available from fiction4all.com in both digital and print editions. His other interests include conspiracy theories, the Knights Templars and has a fascination for the paranormal and supernatural. Which may explain why he wrote 2020-Wipeout a couple of years before Covid-19 had ever been mentioned!

www.ingramcontent.com/pod-product-compliance
Lightning Source LLC
Chambersburg PA
CBHW011501170626
46814CB00008B/2988